Wingman

T0364277

WINGMAN

Elite Ops #2

EMMY CURTIS

New York   Boston

Forever Yours
Hachette Book Group
1290 Avenue of the Americas, New York, NY 10104
forever-romance.com
twitter.com/foreverromance

First published as an ebook and as a print on demand trade paperback: November 2017

Forever Yours is an imprint of Grand Central Publishing. The Forever Yours name and logo are trademarks of Hachette Book Group, Inc.

The publisher is not responsible for websites (or their content) that are not owned by the publisher.

The Hachette Speakers Bureau provides a wide range of authors for speaking events. To find out more, go to www.hachettespeakersbureau.com or call (866) 376-6591.

ISBNs: 978-1-4789-4795-0 (ebook); 978-1-4789-4793-6 (trade paperback)

With love to the Chief . . . No, you're a book.

CHAPTER ONE

Major Missy "Warbird" Malden shifted uncomfortably in her chair and looked around her holding cell. It was pretty clean, all things considered. Not that she'd had much experience with cells, other than those she'd seen on TV. It had been touch and go for a while when she was a kid, but she'd always managed to avoid the cops for the most part, unlike the vast majority of her friends. At least until that one time...She shrugged to herself. At least there wasn't a toilet in the corner.

But clean or not, this was not where she'd thought she would be two days into the Red Flag exercise. She should be up in the skies, directing test missions and worrying about how to explain to her front-seat pilot, Lieutenant Colonel Francis Conrad, why she was requesting a transfer to another squadron—at least in a way that he'd believe. Her heart clenched in her chest as she realized how badly she'd screwed everything up.

At least she didn't have to worry about that conversation anymore. She was pretty sure that being arrested under suspicion of espionage was going to put the brakes on her career. Especially since she couldn't defend herself from the accusation. Or suspicion, or whatever it was that had landed her in jail.

She couldn't understand how a horrible, *horrible* accident had somehow turned into a criminal inquiry within a few hours. And worse, people seemed to think that she was somehow involved. A Royal Air Force pilot, along with Eleanor Daniels—Missy's best friend and roommate at the Red Flag training exercises—were missing in the Nevada desert after both their planes went down. How anyone could even contemplate that Missy had anything to do with such a horrible accident was completely bat-shit crazy. But was it an accident?

Please be alive. Please be alive. The two pilots hadn't been found yet, which she hoped was a good sign. But why couldn't their surveillance locate them? Missy clenched her fists. There was something very off about all this.

Red Flag was supposed to be a safe place to train, a yearly opportunity to finesse skills and beat the shit out of the friendly foreign military pilots who came to train and compete with them. It was basically one big bragging-rights fest with a side order of making or breaking airborne careers.

It was an exercise that was always run with precision. Until this time. When she'd heard that TechGen-One, a military contractor, was sponsoring this year's training, she'd been thrilled. Hell, everyone had, because the whole event had been slated to be canceled due to budget issues.

But since they'd arrived to compete, nothing had gone as expected. And what was more worrying, TGO seemed to have taken operational control of the base in exchange for providing the Red Flag funds, all with the approval of General Daniels, Eleanor's father.

Now it was hard to tell which way was up and whose orders to obey.

The door banged open, and Missy instinctively jumped up. A man in dress blues entered, a thick file beneath one arm. "As you were." He nodded back to her chair.

She sat as was ingrained habit. The silver oak-leaf emblem on his collar told her he was a lieutenant colonel; the name on his badge said "Janke." He outranked her. He loomed large in the doorway, tall and blond, with a buzz cut that made him look more like a marine recruit than an air force officer.

"I've been assigned as your JAG in this matter," he said, flipping open the folder with a pen. Crap. If she'd already been assigned a judge advocate general, the general must really believe she had something to do with the crashes.

Shit just got real. She was legitimately a suspect. Somehow she'd expected that someone would open the door and let her go. Apologize for the mistake. She'd half thought it would be Conrad, the one person on earth who'd go to bat for her. Who'd believe her. Who'd cut through the bullshit and get to the right person with the right information.

He sat at the table, and she followed suit.

"What exactly is it that I'm being accused of? If someone would just tell me, I'm sure I could clear this up pretty quickly." She just wanted to get back to her aircraft, get airborne, and help search for Eleanor and the British pilot.

"Sir," he said.

What? "I'm sorry—"

"You forgot to say *sir*." He leaned back in his chair. "Do you make it a habit of disrespecting your superior officers?"

She frowned. She hadn't come across an officer with that kind of attitude in ten years. She forced her face into a blank expression. "No, sir. I apologize."

He stared at her, his light blue eyes cold, empty almost, and his thin lips pursed together.

A feeling of dread seeped through her, rendering her hands and feet cold. She flexed her fingers.

"All you have to tell us is where you were the night before last." He pulled a tight smile and reopened the file on the table between them. "And tell us anything you know about TechGen-One and General Daniels. Particularly anything Eleanor said."

She fought not to do a double take. *What?* Why was he asking about TechGen-One and Eleanor's father? Suddenly, a whole battery of thoughts whirled in her head. She'd been right. Damn.

"I don't know anything about TGO except what everyone knows, sir. They saved Red Flag from being canceled.

As for General Daniels...I've..." She paused. Why was her lawyer interrogating her?

She put her palms flat on the table. "Colonel Janke. Why don't you tell me what the charges against me are? I mean, you did say you were my assigned JAG, didn't you?" She paused. "Sir." This was total bullshit.

He rose slowly and gave her a smile. A pitying, condescending smile. But even that couldn't disguise the jumping vein in his neck. "This is the moment, Major." He nodded. "This is the moment you will look back on for the rest of your life—no matter how long or short that may be—and you'll wonder if answering my two simple questions would have saved you."

She didn't like the long pause he inserted after the word *short*. She didn't like anything about this. "Are you threatening me, sir?"

He moved fast, banging his fist on the table. She jerked back from him and then cursed herself for showing her fear.

"I don't have to threaten, Major. Your entire future is in my hands." There was a pause—a silence that hung in the air.

Missy forced herself to hold his gaze. "I want a different JAG."

A line wrinkled his forehead, and she was sure she saw a flash of panic in his eyes. He straightened. "Just those two questions, and I'll make sure you'll be back in barracks by sunset."

Her gut told her not to trust him. If being on the streets as a kid had taught her one thing, it was to listen to her gut. "I want a different JAG," she repeated.

He took a step toward her, and she scraped her chair loudly away from the table and stood.

Colonel Janke looked her up and down, not lasciviously, but maybe wondering how much she'd fight back.

She took a step toward him, invading his personal space and forcing him to take one backward. She wanted him to know exactly how she would respond to a threat against her.

Whatever the hell this was turning into, she wasn't going down without a fight.

CHAPTER TWO

48 hours before

Lieutenant Colonel Francis Conrad stretched in front of the hangar, inhaling the clean, warm morning air and listening to the Royal Australian Air Force's music wafting across the runway. No matter how many noise citations they received from Colonel Cameron, the base commander, they never wavered in their mission to give everyone a headache first thing in the morning. What the fuck was a "Waltzing Matilda" anyway?

He rolled his neck, wincing as it cracked in protest. The beds at the Nellis Air Force Base lodging were not known for their comfort.

"At least you had lodging beds, not barrack beds," a voice as familiar as his own said from behind him.

Missy. And then everything was right in his world. He turned and grinned at her. "How do you read my mind like that?" He'd asked her that a thousand times. She anticipated his every move both in and out of the aircraft. It was like she lived in his head. *Not just in my head.*

"I really am just that good," she said, raising her hand for their customary high five. "What's the program today?"

This was their daily routine. He knew very well that she was probably already on top of what they would be doing, but she always allowed him the opportunity to give her instructions. It was a courtesy not many other majors would afford a lieutenant colonel. "Flight briefing, then up into the wild blue yonder...," he said, quoting the U.S. Air Force song with a degree of cheese he found quite dismaying.

"The wild blue yonder, huh?" she said with her hands on her hips "Well, I guess sometimes you do surprise me, Cheese-Meister."

"That's Cheese-Meister, *sir*, to you, Major," he replied, matching her grin.

Missy just rolled her eyes, another thing she did pretty often. "How was the gymnast? Cirque du Soleil?"

"What?" He frowned, not understanding how they jumped from cheese to gymnastics.

"The gymnast," she said, as if he should know what she was talking about. "Oh my God. How have you already forgotten? Women really are just disposable to you, aren't they?"

Shit. He remembered now. He'd told her he'd been with a gymnast when she'd last called him. "No, they are not. I didn't only consider her a gymnast. I considered her"—he eyed Missy's short brunette hair—"a beautiful blonde called..." Oh shit. He looked over Missy's shoulder and saw the flight chief, Sally Weiss. "Sally."

Missy bit her lip and followed his line of sight and saw the chief. "You can't even remember her name, can you?"

It was hard to remember the name of someone who didn't actually exist. He blew out his cheeks and hung his head. To his relief, she laughed.

"Come on, let's get the road on the show." She nodded toward the main administrative building, where they were due to receive their flight brief.

They started walking. "So, where does she work? I mean, is 'gymnast' an actual profession or just a hobby? Is she an Olympian? Does she work in Cirque du Soleil? I've been wanting to see their Vegas show for ages. Was she nice?"

"She was..." He searched for something to say. "Bendy?" *Goddamn it.* Why was he having such trouble lying to her today? He lied to her nearly every day. What made today different?

Missy snorted and shook her head sadly. "One day you'll appreciate a woman's mind, maybe even remember her name, but probably by then you'll be way too old to do anything about it."

"Don't hold your breath. Anyway, I appreciate *your* mind, Mindy. I mean Missy."

She punched him on the arm, like he knew she would. Then she changed the subject. "Have you inspected the aircraft?" she asked.

"Not yet. I'll do that preflight. Why?"

"Eleanor and I couldn't get into the hangar last night.

And then while we waited for someone to remove the lock, the doors opened and some guys came out on a freaking golf cart."

"Jesus. That's not right. Who were they?"

"They wouldn't tell us. Didn't say what they'd been doing either. Eleanor said she was going to talk to her father about it, but I didn't get a good feeling about it at all."

"Okay, no problem. We can do the preflight inspection together. Don't worry." He reached out and gave her head a noogie without actually touching her head.

She batted his hand away as she always did. "I need to talk to you later. Can you save some time for me after the mission debrief?" she asked, head still down as they walked.

"Is everything okay?" His mind spun.

She smiled, but the smile didn't reach her—he wanted to say eyes, but in reality it hadn't really reached her mouth either.

"Sure. After our last flight of the day?" In years of them flying together, she'd never asked for a meeting like that.

She nodded. "Don't worry, though. I won't keep you away from your extracurricular ladies for too long."

"So funny. So, so funny. Listen. Can you hear? My ribs are actually cracking because I'm laughing so hard," he deadpanned. He sneaked a quick look at her to see if he could glean anything from her expression. All he could see were the morning rays reflected in her sunglasses.

* * *

She'd done it. She'd actually made a firm appointment to speak to him. Now she had to figure out what to say that wouldn't leave him thinking she was hopelessly in love with him. Not that she was, but if she wasn't careful, she was pretty sure that was all he'd take away from the conversation.

Well, maybe she was. God, life was so difficult. Why couldn't she have been the weapons officer for Lieutenant Colonel Walsh? He was smart, married to a wonderful woman, and had kids he doted on. He was funny too. In a kind of 1990s sit-com way. Maybe more of a groan-at-his-jokes way.

Sitting behind Conrad day in, day out, anticipating his every move, working so closely that she could read his body language from behind him, not to mention being able to smell his shower gel mingling with his own unique scent, had become pure torture.

She had to get away. She couldn't—didn't want to—change their relationship. There was no legit way to do anything about the feelings she had for him. If she made the first move and he rejected her, he could report her for behavior unbecoming. If he didn't reject her, they could both be fired for fraternization. It was a lose-lose proposition that was making her crazy. And that had to stop.

Besides which, Conrad was with a different woman every night. She'd spent nights wondering what he looked like under his uniform and her days wondering why he needed to bed so many women. *So. Many.*

Her heart wanted to be closer to him in every way, but her brain had finally come to the realization that he wasn't going to change. He wasn't going to suddenly wake up and see what was under his nose. And her dating life had suffered for it.

When she'd first met him, she compared every date to him. Now she just didn't date, and that was bad. Everyone told her that she needed something other than work and her horses. She didn't necessarily agree, but the one thing she could figure out for herself was that staying around Conrad wasn't going to further her career or help her find someone to share her life with.

Transferring to a different squadron was the only option. Out of sight, out of mind. And hopefully it would put half the country between them. She needed to get on with her life, find someone who liked her, and give dating a chance. Anything but be stuck in this painful limbo. She needed a life. A fucking fun life.

The flight briefing was fast, because all the F-15 weapons officers were in charge of planning the strategic mission, while the pilots just got them to their destination. In real terms, up in the air, she was the mission commander and he was the aircraft commander.

Their mission this morning was to deploy with the French Air Force and to bomb an unknown moving target. The U.S. Aggressor Squadron would be tasked with trying to stop them. Which meant they'd be flying against her barracks roommate, Eleanor Daniels. Missy grinned, her head firmly in the game. Eleanor was totally buying the drinks tonight if she and Conrad hit the target. And they would. Failure was not an option for either of them. That was at least one thing they agreed on. Conrad and Missy had never been "shot down" at Red Flag before, and today wouldn't be any different.

Besides which, she would probably need a drink after the conversation she had to have with him later. Eleanor would understand, and join her.

But for now, Missy had to keep her laser focus. It had become harder and harder to compartmentalize. Conrad was a work colleague. Nothing more. She just had to complete this Red Flag, and she would have a new life and a fighting chance at a real future.

She suited up and made her way to the flight line, where all the U.S. Air Force planes were chocked, awaiting departure. She instantly recognized Conrad in the distance. Not that she could see his face, but she knew the way he walked and how he held himself: head up, one hand trailing on the aircraft's fuselage, and one hand tapping against the outside of his thigh. He tapped his leg every time he checked something. She wondered if he was mentally reciting a mnemonic but had never asked.

"Everything look okay to you?" she asked, switching her helmet from one hand to the other as she grabbed the ladder to climb into her seat.

"Everything looks fine. No dings, no scrapes—she looks as beautiful as she always does."

She smiled. "Good." She'd been a little worried since the previous night. But if Conrad said it was in working order, she 100 percent believed him. Damn stupid civilians with their stupid golf cart. She cursed under her breath at the thought. Just a tiny ding could damage the airworthiness of a plane . . . and cause unspeakably bad crashes.

Missy took a deep breath and got into flight mode. She slipped a bandana around her hairline to stop sweat from dripping into her eyes or onto her instruments and fastened her helmet securely in place. Her heartbeat flicked up a notch, and she smiled. She'd always told herself she'd give up the job when she failed to feel the small shiver of preflight excitement that tickled her spine every time she slid into her seat.

She couldn't, however, bring herself to avert her eyes as Conrad slipped into his. His ass was a work of art. It would be virtually rude not to admire it. At least that was what she'd been telling herself for years now. Shaking her head to herself with a private smile, she checked her instruments and her comms.

"Do you copy?" she said

"I certainly do," Conrad replied with an audible smile and an exaggerated Southern accent. *Ah certain-lay do.* The boy was from Savannah, Georgia, and his redneck charm was what they said made him so popular with women. She couldn't disagree.

She let him run through his preflight check, affirming

each question that pertained to her. It was such a routine that she had to totally focus to ensure she wasn't just going through the motions. She snapped a rubber band against her wrist as she checked her own instruments and weaponry. It kept her focused, and thankfully, no one could see her doing it and imagine that she was trying to distract herself from what voices were telling her to do. She grinned at the thought. Conrad would crap himself if someone told him that the woman sitting behind him at twenty thousand feet was snapping a rubber band on her wrist.

In truth, it just made her focus and helped take away any distraction or her predisposition to think ahead. It was a part of her flight routine that one of her in- structors had passed on in her training. She had started her weapons officer training trying to think three steps ahead until the trainer had told them all that they had to stay utterly focused on the one thing that was hap- pening at that moment. Her rubber band had become like a talisman, and a reminder that her training was all that mattered.

Conrad started the engines and they awaited the crew sergeant on the ground to give the signs that the chocks had been removed. There was a momentary engine whine as he throttled forward, and she nodded to the sergeant who saluted them as they left the stand.

Soon enough they were accelerating down the runway, through the heat waves hovering above the tarmac. One day maybe she'd be able to just sit and enjoy the ride, but as always, she was swiveling her head to get a visual on other aircraft in the pattern and inputting coordinates for the mission.

"We've got Stone Man on our six. Suggest we hold in a pattern over Guardian Lake for the others to catch up," she said.

Conrad was banking left toward the lake before she'd finished her sentence. They needed to fly to their target in formation. It was a good place to await the other pilots, especially if there was a delay in takeoff.

As they were circling the lake, she watched as a beautiful British Typhoon soared into the sky. "Look at that," she said with a sigh. As Conrad's head swiveled, the plane banked to the right, away from them, giving them a spectacular view of its undercarriage with its camo paint and Royal Air Force target-shaped roundel design on its wings. "She's beautiful."

"I'm hurt. So is *Lana*. Don't let her know you're ogling another aircraft," Conrad replied. Only he would name his aircraft after a sexy cartoon spy.

"*Lana* can take the hit. I'm not sure your ego can, though," she replied with a laugh. "Maybe you can introduce me to the pilot when we're on the ground?" she said, not meaning it at all. This was the game they played. Or she played at least. It made her feel better about all the gymnasts, exotic dancers, and nurses Conrad spent his off-duty hours with.

"I don't know every pilot at Red Flag, you know." His voice had taken an edge of outrage that made her grin.

"Well, if you cared about me at all, you'd be scoping out all the single pilots and screening them for me."

He was silent, and she scanned her instruments and the sky around her for a reason he wasn't replying to her. There was nothing out there except another French pilot joining their holding pattern. "Well?"

He cleared his throat. "If you want me to pimp for you, I'm certainly happy to. I'll go find him after our chat." His voice had put air quotes around the word *chat*, making it seem like an imposition.

"Thank you," she said, wondering why she'd pushed him. Hopefully the British pilot was married.

This. This was what her life had become. They'd chitchat until one of them said something that would give the other ass ache; then it would be weird. She swore that she spent half the time trying to figure out what she'd said to make him clam up or straight-up get annoyed at. It wasn't natural—especially since from day to day he was often the only man she spent any time with. It was unhealthy. Hell, the whole thing was unhealthy. And that's why she needed to get out of Dodge.

His head flicked to the right, and that coupled with a change in the engine vibration told her they were ready to go. Before he'd even said anything, she was giving him the radar reading on their route to the target. "We've got turbulence between seventeen and twenty-one thousand feet," she reminded him. "And our fastest way there is skimming around Mount Irish Wilderness, keeping Bald Mountain on our port side."

"Copy that," he said, repeating the route on the frequency for their sortie. All the other pilots clicked in, acknowledging the instructions.

She propped her left arm up on the small ledge where the canopy met the airframe to give herself a little more space. She watched the radar for other aircraft movements and checked and double-checked the missiles they were carrying below them. They weren't dropping real missiles until the last few days of Red Flag; they just had flares loaded for now.

Missy could close her eyes and tell immediately who she was flying with. Some pilots embraced the turbulence, some tried to avoid it for her sake—because it was bumpier toward the rear of the aircraft—and some accelerated and decelerated, trying to get the perfect vector on a target, making her head bob back and forth.

Conrad embraced the turbulence. Which meant that she had to as well. And sometimes she wished the rattling would shake some sense into him, but it never did. The turbulence kept him sharp, and she always wondered if that's why he fought stability in his personal life too. Entanglements dulled the instincts, as common wisdom held.

He called out direction to their sortie. "We're coming in north, northeast. Aggressor Squadron is directly ahead on the radar, so let's take flanking positions on the target to spread them out."

Conrad dipped *Lana*'s wing, and the engines roared as he punched forward toward the fight. That's what he always did. No strategizing, no hiding, just jumping right into the fray.

CHAPTER THREE

The mission had been a success, but Conrad couldn't figure out what was wrong with Missy. She'd been having some kind of tizzy since they'd arrived at Red Flag. She'd been different, standoffish—like he'd maybe done something to upset her. He just couldn't figure out what.

He'd done everything he was supposed to. He could say that he'd pushed her away, but she'd never really got that close to him. Never given him the slightest impression that would have legitimized the need that burned inside him.

And thank God. Sometimes he knew that his rampant desire for her would have totally taken him over if she'd even looked at him a certain way. He needed to get his head back in the game. He'd missed her after their last flight of the day because the crew chief needed to speak to him. But he couldn't just hang out and wait for her to be ready to tell him what the fuck was up.

He swung by the barracks to find her, but Major Eleanor Daniels, Missy's roommate, told him that she'd gone to the gym. So be it.

He changed into his PT clothes at his lodging and headed down to the base gym. As he expected, it was virtually deserted except for a few guys doing weights and Missy punching a bag.

"Oh, come on. Today wasn't *that* bad," he joked as he took in the ferocity with which she was victimizing the bag.

She paused, blew hair out of her eyes, and put her hands on her hips. "Where did you go? I waited for you in the briefing room."

He frowned. This sounded serious. "The crew chief wanted to talk to me about something they found on one of the F-16s. I came to find you right after, which is why I'm here." He definitely wasn't going to mention the lipstick graffiti that had been left for Eleanor on the side of her aircraft. He hoped it had just been a prank. In bad taste, for sure. Lipsticking *Bitch* was bordering on criminal. He hoped Eleanor hadn't seen it. Something like that was designed to get into someone's head, throw them off their game. Whoever had done it didn't have the balls to compete on a level playing field. If Conrad found the bastard who'd written it, he'd be toast.

Missy nodded toward the punching bag and he took hold of it to give her a better target. She hit it over and over, as if she was shivving someone in jail. Hard and fast. Really fast. He planted his feet farther apart to counter the thrust on the bag.

"Dude. What's wrong?" he asked.

She stopped and wiped sweaty hair from her forehead with the back of her boxing glove. "I've asked for a transfer to MacDill."

His brain stuttered at her bald statement. "What?" She couldn't just leave him and live on the other side of the country.

"It's time."

"It's time for what?" he ground out, trying not to sound upset and failing miserably.

"I've learned all I can from you...and the other pilots I fly with. It's time for me to press on, or I'll be in this squadron for another year at least. No one wants that." She smiled as if she was making a weak joke.

His brain couldn't process what she was saying. In the years they'd been in the same squadron, never once had he contemplated being without her. Not being able to fly with her. Not seeing her every day. It had never even...even crossed his mind. *Shit.*

He laughed, unable to figure out what to say, and her face froze.

"Why are you laughing?" she said. The expression that had been on her face while she'd been punching the bag returned. He stepped back.

"I don't know." He held his hands up. "I'm sorry. It's just so unexpected. I assumed you—"

"You assumed that I'd just stay flying with you until you decided to move on to another job, right?"

He shrugged. "Yeah, I mean—"

She stepped back and took a breath. He waited for her to say something, his mind whirring...how could she not see that he wouldn't be as good a pilot if she wasn't sitting behind him? How could she not see that she was changing their lives without even consulting him?

She said nothing. But her face reflected some kind of recognition or understanding.

Relieved, he exhaled heavily. "You see? It's okay. You can take back a request for transfer. I can ask Colonel Bailey to ignore it. It'll be fine." Thank God she realized her mis—

She punched him in the soft spot of his shoulder, just over his collarbone.

He rubbed it and grabbed the bag again. "You missed it." He smirked.

She pushed him with both hands and he was propelled backward toward the mats.

"What are you doing?" *What the fuck is going on?*

She advanced on him again and pushed him, making him almost trip on the corner of the gym mat. He held up his hands in surrender. "All right, Missy. Calm down."

She hung her head for a second, and he put both his hands on her shoulders. She looked up, forced his hands away from her, and grabbed one of his arms and pulled him toward her, while blocking his legs from moving with her right leg. Effortlessly she threw him over her left hip. Boom. He landed on the mat. *Damn.*

A couple of the guys doing weights sniggered. Awesome.

He propped himself up on his elbows. "Are we done now? Is this all sorted now?"

"Are you kidding me?" she asked. "You have no idea how to even be a human being. How to think about anyone other than yourself."

Well that wasn't true. He thought about her all the fucking time. About what he wanted to do with her, about kissing her—she just didn't understand. He whipped his legs around to the side and tripped her. "What exactly is going on here?"

She fell to the left of him, but so close he felt the breath poof out of her as she fell. He jumped up and held his hand out to her. She ignored it, getting to her feet herself, and charged him from a crouching position, using her weight below his center of gravity to hit him back to the mat.

This time she landed on top of him. She held his gaze for a couple of seconds, and then scrambled to get off him. He held her firmly by the arms. "I'm not your punching bag. Whatever you have going on—"

"Then what exactly am I to you? Just some person whose only job is to make you look good up there? Your...sidekick?" She bucked against his arms, managing to get a knee to his groin, but thankfully missing all the important parts. He roared and spun her onto her back.

Before she fully made contact with the mat, she spun away and leapt to her feet. Crap, but she was slippery when she was pissed. He realized in that instant that he'd never seen her pissed. Or even sad or ecstatic. Around him, she'd always been in work mode. Professional, a little sardonic, occasionally lighthearted.

One of the lights went out in the gym, and he looked toward the weight machine and realized everyone had left, presumably to go party downtown, as most people did when they were in Vegas. In his moment of distraction, he had only a split second to react to a kick to his chest. Reeling from the impact, he still managed to grab her foot and hold it up.

"Well, I've got you n—" he started.

She bent her remaining floor-bound leg and sprung. A second foot caught him in his chest and he went down. As did she, gratifyingly.

He had no idea why they were fighting, but as he lay there, catching his breath, he realized that he'd never touched her like this before. Never held her arms, never laid that close to her. He took a breath, during which he pleaded with every ounce of willpower in his body to not get a hard-on.

"Get up," Missy said. He'd been concentrating so hard on his dick that he hadn't noticed that she was already on her feet.

What was going on? He needed to get the fuck out of here . . .

"Get up." He looked up. She was standing next to him, hands firmly planted on her hips.

"Are we still fighting?" he asked, trying not to let the

strain show in his voice. He rolled over and sat up, hiding the bulge in his shorts with a casually slung arm.

"You can. I'm heading for the shower," she said, holding her hand out.

At that image, his self-control fritzed and everything in his life faded except the woman in front of him. He took her hand, as if he were going to get up, and pulled her down to him.

A cry of surprise echoed around the empty gym as she fell on him. Full-body contact. *Full*-body contact.

She wriggled as if to get up, and then she paused. And then wriggled a tiny bit more. "What's that?" She pulled her head up and stared at him, a frown marring her beautiful face.

He hesitated, once again in the real world. He should push her off him. Apologize, and head back to his—

She pushed her pelvis against his hard-on. He closed his eyes and groaned. And then it was game over.

He opened his eyes and pulled her toward him, rolling so that he was on top of her. "Tell me to stop," he said. "Just say the word, but say it now."

She opened her mouth but said nothing. Her eyes trailed down his face and rested on his mouth. She took a shaky breath. He was afraid of what she was going to say, but she remained silent.

In that second, his body acted before his brain. He was going to say something—something clever, or cute maybe. Or sexy. But instead he pulled her to him and kissed her. She utterly yielded beneath him. Her mouth opened, and her tongue dueled with his. Heat—pure volcanic heat—rushed through him as he took what he had wanted for so long. What she was finally giving him.

It was wrong, so very wrong. But nothing could tell his soul that she was wrong for him. Nothing could convince his crazed need for her to fit neatly back into its flight suit. It was out.

Her back arched against the pressure of his lips and teeth on her neck. And then she stiffened. He pulled back immediately. Sanity rushed into his head.

"Fuck," he said, rolling her off him and staring at the ceiling light. "I'm sorry. I just—I don't have an excuse. It shouldn't have happened, and I apologize." His chest heaved under the intensity of the kiss and the immense feat of willpower it had taken to push her away.

She took a breath, and he turned his head to hear what she had to say. But she just stared at him before getting up and running to the locker room.

Fuck. What had he done? He lay there, wondering what the fuck was going on. The one constant in his life had gone nuts, and then kissed him, and now his whole world had changed. He'd kissed her. Felt her body under his.

Nothing would be the same now.

What had she done? Missy had run back to the barracks and stepped into the shower as if the water could wash away what she'd just done. She'd fucking kissed him. It felt like some kind of self-betrayal.

It was so confusing. Kissing him was . . . It had scared her. She'd never seen him lose control like that. Never witnessed him act on anything other than precision and professionalism. But it was bad. Bad that she'd liked it so much. Bad that she hadn't wanted it to stop. The one thing that *had* stopped her was her realization that in all the years they'd flown together, he totally considered her a sidekick. There only to make him look good, to make his life easier.

And as she realized that he only saw her as an extension of him, it was as if a curtain had been parted, shedding light for the first time into a dusty room. He didn't know anything about her. He'd never asked her about her family—not that she would ever have wanted to go there—or her friends. He'd never even asked her where she was from, what movies she liked—nothing. He'd never gone out socially with her, and now that she was putting all these things together, she was furious with herself for wasting two years of her life pining for him.

Assuming no one would match up to the awesomeness that was Conrad. What utter fuckery.

It was a bitter discovery. Conrad was, and always had been, just about himself.

And now, goddamn it, she'd betrayed herself in one stupid moment of anger and passion. She winced as she thought the word *passion*, but that was how she'd always thought about him.

As for him, he probably just wanted another conquest. Judging by his endless revolving door of women, he probably had a hard-on for every female he came across.

She'd fucked everything up—but that made her even more determined to move on, to get away from this situation that was fast becoming more and more toxic. The transfer was legit. It was the right thing to do. She couldn't stay.

Missy stepped out of the shower and wrapped a towel around her head. Sinking onto the foot of the bed, she touched her lips, where he had touched her with his. They felt...plundered. His kiss, their fight, the feeling of his hardness against her...God, but her libido had kicked in so damned fast.

Hell, no. She wasn't Monday-morning-quarterbacking this one. She had to shake it off. Forget it.

Her phone rang. *Conrad.* Shit. She took two deep breaths and picked up the call. "Hello?" She was proud of how even and normal her voice sounded.

"Hey. Look. Can you come get me before you go back to the hangar? We can talk on the way. We...need to..."

"Talk?" she said, enjoying his discomfort.

He sighed. "Yes. We will talk all night about it, because if we have to sleep on those god-awful cots in the hangar, I'm going to make it as uncomfortable and awkward as possible for everyone. Because that's the way I roll," he said.

She laughed. She hated hangar duty, but after the people meddling in there the previous night, she was never going to complain about it again. If she had to sleep in the hangar to make sure her aircraft wasn't touched by anyone else, then that was what she'd do.

"Sure. But if you think you're going to make me feel awkward, you better bring it, because I can tell you about girl stuff that'll gross you out and make you squirm," she said. And then she realized that *squirm* could be taken more than one way. She rolled her eyes at herself in the mirror.

He sounded as if he were choking down the phone. "Room 2123."

"I'll be there." She ended the call.

She slumped back on the bed. At least he'd seemed a little more himself. And she was going to be totally professional too. She was leaving the squadron, and that was it. She didn't need to feel bad, or explain it to anyone, let alone him. Taking several deep breaths, she relaxed.

She could forget the kiss, the burning intensity of his gaze. The weight of him on top of her, the way she had involuntarily arched against him. Closing her eyes, she could visualize him. Her body started to replicate the heat and need that had coursed through her when he'd asked her to tell him no. She'd had every intention of saying no, but her mouth and the air in her lungs refused to cooperate. There was no one in the world who could have said no right there and right then. No one. Least of all her.

But it was a momentary lapse. It was not going to happen again, regardless of how her body had melted into his.

She was tempted to touch herself. To finish what he'd started. But that was no way to move past it. No way to get over him. No way to make a clean break. And she was determined to get away in one piece.

She needed a career that wasn't dependent on the one person who made it impossible to have a personal life. God, she wished there was alcohol in their room. She checked the mini-fridge in case Eleanor had left some. Nope.

There was nothing else to do but press on, address the "kiss" and get over it. She blew out a puff of air as she chose some clothes to wear for the evening. Yoga pants, a tank top, and a sweatshirt for when it got cold. She bundled her Kindle, phone, and flashlight into a tote and strode out of the room with her shoulders squared and her head up. She was going to face him with no embarrassment and no fear. She had nothing to lose.

As she left the barracks, Sergeant Cripps was going in. He raised a hand. He opened his mouth to say something, but she interrupted him, knowing full well what he was going to ask.

"Yup. Absolutely. Colonel Conrad and I are on our way now."

"Thank you, ma'am," he replied, holding the door open for her.

"Have a good eve...night," she said, casting her gaze to the already darkening sky.

"You too, ma'am," he replied.

"Just how likely do you think that will be?" she asked, thinking about the metal cots the crew put up for the watcher shift.

"Not too likely, ma'am," he said with a grin. "We made your beds up for you, though."

"Thank you. Now you go have a good time sleeping in your regular comfortable bed and leave me alone to my misery." She rolled her eyes with a smile and ran down the steps to the street.

She looked both ways as she crossed the street to the base lodging—essentially a hotel where the senior officers got to stay during Red Flag. As she reached the sidewalk, someone bumped into her. She apologized without seeing who it was, too busy trying to figure out how not to blush when she saw Conrad.

"No, it's my bad. Oh, hey, don't I know you from somewhere?" he said.

She stopped, jolted out of her thoughts. She turned and saw a man with long hair and really white, perfectly formed teeth—the type that were clearly implants. He held out his hand and automatically she took it. He shook it and grasped her shoulder as he did.

It was the man who had been in their hangar the previous night. He squeezed her hand hard. "Nice to meet you," she said, taking her hand and arm back. She fought the impulse to shake her hand to get the feeling back in it. It was a good thing she was wearing a sweatshirt because she was fairly sure that she'd have been skeeved out by him touching her skin.

"We know each other, right?" he persisted. His tone made her wary for some reason. She listened to her gut.

"No, we don't. I'm sorry—I have to go," she said, turning away. She ran up the few steps to the hotel and looked back at him. He was still staring at her, but this time he had a phone to his ear. That was . . . weird.

She found Conrad's room and knocked on the door. It opened.

"Hey. Is it that time already?" Conrad said with an easy smile—almost as if nothing had happened.

"I guess," she said, trying hard not to let her gaze skate away from him. She didn't want to appear shifty or awkward.

He leaned down to pick up a backpack and turned to the small table to reach for his key card.

The elevator doors binged as they opened in the middle of the corridor. She looked to see who had gotten off, just so she wouldn't be looking at Conrad in his faded T-shirt and absurdly well-fitting jeans. The warm, humid mist from the shower he'd obviously just taken emanated from his room, sending his unique scent out into the hallway, almost begging her to step into his lair.

The man who stepped off the elevator looked the other way down the corridor. It was the guy from outside. *Oh God.*

Without thinking, she rushed the few steps into Conrad's room and closed the door so he wouldn't see her. In the process, she ran straight into Conrad, almost pushing him off balance.

He wrapped his arms around her. "Okay, that works too," he said, regaining his balance from her surprise breach.

CHAPTER FOUR

He'd been all set to apologize. To call for calm. To urge her to pretend that kiss had never happened. It was the right thing to do. It was the sane thing to do.

But she just barreled in, throwing herself at him, and he for one wasn't going to look a gift horse in the mouth. Nope. He was going to do something else with that mouth he'd been fantasizing about for years.

He pulled her closer and put his mouth over hers. As he closed his eyes, he clocked a look of bewilderment on her face, but by the time he'd processed it, he was already kissing her, and nothing short of an act of God was going to stop him.

She tensed and he summoned all his willpower to step away from her. But she melted against him before he could, touching every part of her to every part of him, and wrapped her arms around his neck.

Yes. He mentally pumped his fist in the air. She wanted him. She wanted him like fuck, man. Everything he'd been longing for, suffering through those lonely nights for, those cold showers . . . it was all right here, in this room.

He bent his knees and lifted her off the floor. Her legs wrapped around his waist, but he hesitated before turning to put her on the bed. This was as close to heaven as he could imagine, having her wrapped around him. Heat rose in him, and desire turned his whole world into static, the only clarity being the woman he held.

He wrapped his arms around her as if he were trying to absorb her into his body. Just for a second he wanted to assimilate, close his eyes and recognize that she was his, that she'd stay with him now, and they'd fly together until they retired.

He gently bent down and placed her on the bed, not wanting to have her body away from his. She sat on the edge, looking up at him, her brown eyes looking like little eclipsed suns.

He took off his T-shirt and knelt before her on the floor. He opened his mouth to speak, to ask if she was okay with...whatever was about to happen. But she placed a finger over his lips and shook her head. She didn't want to have the conversation.

It was a shame, as her conversation and her fast-as-hell mind always made him slightly dizzy with wanting her. But they could talk later. Would *have* to talk later.

She pushed him away and stood. Her eyes firmly on his, she took off her sweatshirt and her black yoga pants.

His brain became fogged with need as she peeled off her tank top to leave her in peach-colored bra and panties. The shade emphasized her tan skin. He wanted to know when she'd been out in the sun, but his mind had already moved on to the fantasy of her sunbathing in a tiny bikini.

He crowded her, his leg pressing against hers so she fell backward onto the bed. As she lay there, looking up at him, he undid his pants and slid them off.

His dick sprang free, and he took pleasure in watching her gaze follow it. Then he climbed onto the bed next to her and kissed her stomach.

She arched against the touch of his mouth, stretching her arms above her head. He sat up and snaked a hand beneath her, unclipping her bra gratifyingly quickly. She laughed. "Nifty. You've done that before."

"Beginner's luck," he said, trying not to smile.

She crossed her eyes at him, and he gave in to a laugh. He sat astride her, reveling in the feeling of her soft stomach against his dick. He spanned her rib cage with his hands and stroked them upward, until they were under the silky fabric of her bra.

Missy's laugh turned into a moan and his fingers found her nipples. He felt them harden under his fingers and the sensation pushed lava through his veins from his fingertips to his dick. His balls tightened against her. Jesus. Why had he waited so long for this?

She placed an arm over her eyes as if it were too bright in the room, so he switched off the bedside lamps. Although the sun hadn't completely set, the room was rendered into darkness.

With firm hands, she pulled him down on top of her.

And then his body was pressed to hers and the world as he perceived it ceased to exist. Thought escaped him as his body and various fantasies took over.

He swallowed hard against the wave of...something unfamiliar and intense washing over him. Missy was naked, her body pressed against his. He needed to feel her, properly, and he couldn't while he was on top of her. He shifted off her, pulling her with him, so they lay facing each other. He stroked her back from her neck to her shoulders, her waist, and her ass, reveling in the disbelief and wonder that his hands—his own hands—were actually touching Missy's naked body.

Just as he was settling into a haze of need, she pulled away and climbed on top of him. *Ahhh Jesus.* He wished he'd left the lights on. He'd give a million dollars to be able to see her in full freaking Technicolor, naked and astride him. But instead he allowed his eyes to adjust to the shadows, and used his fingers to feel her soft curves and the firm muscles quivering beneath her tan skin. He longed to feel her wetness against his dick. She shifted her pelvis against him in response, and he wondered if she was reading his mind, as she did when they were on duty.

A groan shuddered through him as she opened her legs and slicked along his length. She was so hot and wet and soft. She brought her legs up either side of his hips and pressed her wet heat down on his dick. Her eyes closed as she sat upright and slid herself back and forth along his length.

Then she raised herself off him, causing an unwelcome coolness where her body should have been, and slid her hands over his dick—up and down and in a spiral around the head. He was not going to last worth a damn if she carried on.

"Condom?" she asked, her hand stilling on him.

He tried to gather his senses. "Of course." He pointed to his pilot case and tried to reach it, not wanting Missy to move a fucking inch away from him.

She stifled a laugh at his expression, which probably had an air of desperation about it, and gave him her hand. "I've got it. Anchor me."

For a split second he wondered if that was some kind of sex that he'd missed while pining for Missy from afar. Then he realized she just wanted him to hold her hand so she didn't fall off the bed. He grabbed her hand and she stretched to reach the bag, just being able to drag it toward the bed with her fingertips.

"We're a great team," he said, reaching for the condom.

As soon as the words were out of his mouth, he noticed a slight change in her demeanor. He shouldn't have said that. Wasn't that what their whole argument had been about?

"It's okay," she said. "I'm saving that one to kick you with later."

Dammit, she always fucking knew what he was thinking. All he wanted to do was lose himself in her again.

"Now, where were we?" she asked as if she were inside

his head again. She pulled his dick toward her, until his tip was touching her clit. His eyes widened as he sought to take in this image: Missy, naked, pleasuring herself with his dick. Never had he allowed himself to ever imagine that his fantasies would become real.

And then she placed him at her entrance and moved her hips around in a circle, allowing less than an inch of him inside her. Instinctively, his hands flew to her hips to try to stop her from teasing him before he'd had a chance to put the condom on. But she cocked a confident smile and continued playing with him. He wasn't getting enough of her; he wanted to be balls deep in her, feeling every muscle contract around him.

But also, more than anything, he wanted to see her face when she came. A shot of abject desire stabbed through him, making every muscle in his body contract. He pulled his dick away from her and urged her closer, wanting to make her feel the same need that was pulsing through him.

His fingers plundered her wetness, touching her clit for the first time, making her gasp. The sounds she made nearly pushed him over the edge. The moans and sighs. If he lived to be a hundred, he would never forget how she sounded.

He slid his fingers inside her, almost dying at her heat and wetness and the tightness that stretched around them. She rocked against him, and when he curled his fingers inside and stroked her clit with his thumb, she trembled.

Her head stretched back and he had her. Her nipples puckered for him as if attached to her clit with an invisible wire. He ached to get his mouth on them, but she was so close to coming, he didn't want to stop the momentum. He was in a fucking dream.

She tightened around his fingers, as one last throaty moan filled the room. She came with a rush of loud breaths and spasms, her eyes still closed. He slipped the condom on, and she found his dick immediately, and before he could protest—as if he would—he was inside her. All her heat and wetness surrounded him as she sat firmly down, burying him deep within her.

Lights prickled his peripheral vision. She rode him long and slow, and then faster, seemingly anticipating every nerve ending's demand, until his fists were wound in the bedcover as he strained into her. His balls tightened almost painfully as he exploded inside her. His brain fritzed as if he were concussed. But there was no pain, just amazing release...as if everything in him was reaching out to be a part of her.

"Jesus. Jesus," he said, gasping for air.

She released a small exhale of a laugh before collapsing onto him, with her head on his chest. He stroked her hair and closed his eyes. Her breathing became steady, and he let go, once again, to heaven.

CHAPTER FIVE

It was late—or maybe it was early. Missy rolled over in the darkness and stretched. Then she snapped her arms back in to her body as she realized where she was and who she was with. Shit. The night came flooding back. She looked at his sleeping face. The face that until last night had been that of a colleague. Now everything had changed.

She wanted to smile, but her face wouldn't let her. It was a sadness that descended through her bones. This was illegal. They could both get fired for it. Their careers would be ended—just because they couldn't keep it in their pants.

But also, could this be her closure? She knew him well enough to know that she was just Tuesday's entertainment. He would be on to someone else tomorrow, or maybe the next day. She knew that. And she wouldn't let it hurt when he did.

Casual and breezy, that's what she had to show him.

This was it—closure. She would just have to make sure her transfer paperwork was finalized. There was no way she could let what had just happened influence her decision to stay. And she knew just how persuasive Conrad could be.

But right now? She had to get out of the lodging while everyone was still asleep. How could she look in his eyes again? See him without remembering?

Damn, girl. You've got to get your shit together. She slid out of the bed, grabbed her clothes, and took them to the bathroom.

She switched on the light and checked her phone. It was 4:00 a.m. Just time enough to get back to the barracks before Eleanor awoke. Conrad had virtually fucked away her brain power, enough that she couldn't quickly come up with a reason she'd been out this long. Especially dressed the way she was.

Fuck! They were supposed to have been in the hangar last night. *Shit-fuck.* Briefly she contemplated waking Conrad and getting them both the hell down there. But she didn't want to talk to him about this shit yet. Hell on wheels.

She made up her mind. She'd slip out of lodging, head to the hangar, ruffle up their cots, and then run back to barracks in time to get in the shower before Eleanor awoke.

She walked through the reception area with her head down, in case anyone she knew from the other squadrons was there. But it was deserted, thank God.

As soon as she hit the street, she ran along white lines

in the center of the empty road as she always did. That was the beauty of the base here. They redirected traffic in the mornings so troops could do their PT without getting run over.

She banked right onto the flight line and kept running until she reached the F-15 and F-16 hangar. The door was unlocked, of course, so she slipped right in. It was completely dark except for the ambient light coming from the mechanics' office on the mezzanine level. Someone had left a computer running probably.

She found their cots on either side of their F-15. She stopped and steadied her breath. Was there someone there? She spun around, only to see the shadows of the aircraft pulled into the hangar, nose to tail, wingtip to wingtip. She held her breath to see if she could sense the air moving around an intruder.

But no. There was no one. She mussed up her own cot, scrunching the pillow and pulling the blankets back, and was about to do Conrad's, too, but, with an evil smile to herself, decided to hang him out to dry and see what excuse he'd come up with when the crew asked him why he hadn't slept in the hangar. The thought of him struggling to find a good answer made her giggle to herself. Poor Conrad. Of course, he didn't have to explain himself to anyone, but she knew the crew would ask. She just hoped she'd be around to see him blush.

Looking around one more time, she picked her way carefully around the aircraft, ducking under their wings.

There was no one there. She was going mad. She blamed Conrad for her brain being on the fritz. Taking one last look around, she bailed, closing the door quietly behind her and running back to her barracks.

"Well, well, well," Eleanor said as soon as Missy opened the door to their shared quarters. "I never imagined to catch you doing the walk of shame at this hour. Don't you know you're supposed to be in the air in a few hours?"

"Shhhhh!" Missy said, closing the door quietly behind her. She figured no one else on their floor would be waking up for another hour or so.

Eleanor was sitting in the one armchair in the room, with her PC on her lap. "Help yourself to a cup of coffee." She nodded toward the pot on top of the small fridge.

Missy dumped her bag on her bed and went to pour the coffee.

"Oh my God, you totally got laid," Eleanor gasped, closing her laptop.

"What? How do... Why would you say that?" Missy stumbled unconvincingly over her words.

"You just sashayed across the room. And unless you're doing it for my benefit..."

Missy went on the offensive. "Well, what are you doing up so early, wearing the same clothes—" She broke off. "Oh my God, so did you!"

They stared at each other for a second, then burst out laughing. Missy raised her coffee cup in a salute.

"Here's to deepening international relations with our

NATO partners," Eleanor said with a grin, lifting her own cup in response.

"Really? With a foreign national? You rebel!"

Eleanor just raised her eyebrows lasciviously and tucked her feet under her. "Are you going to tell Conrad?" she asked.

Missy winced.

"Oh my God!" Eleanor shouted before clapping her hand over her mouth. "Seriously? That's...I don't know what that is. Wonderful? Career-ending?"

Missy took a deep breath. "Closure. That's what it is."

"Are you sure? Are you still requesting your transfer?" she asked.

"Now more than ever," Missy replied firmly. She was completely convinced that she'd made the right decision. Getting out from under Conrad's career path and forging her own and doing it with at least three states between them sounded like a good plan to her.

"What does Conrad think?"

Missy took a deep breath, trying to suppress the rage she'd felt earlier. "He feels that I should stay with him until he's reached his own personal career goals."

Eleanor nodded thoughtfully.

Missy was a little pissed that she wasn't more outraged on her behalf.

"I can't honestly say I blame him. You're the best weapons officer in his squadron. You read his mind, can anticipate his every operational need, and if I flew an F-15 and needed someone in the backseat, I'd want to hold on to you as long as possible."

"No. I'm sorry. You can't bring your reason and stupid pilot-logic to a personal grudge."

"You're right. He's an arrogant prick, and I hate him. But all pilots are, you know." Eleanor shrugged and gazed at her cup of coffee.

"You're not," Missy said.

"Yes, I am. You just haven't flown with me. I'm the worst, but I have to be. Otherwise those flyboys will stomp all over my mad skills, even though I'm a much better pilot than they are." She grinned.

"You are right—you *are* an arrogant prick."

Silence fell between them for a second. Missy hoped they'd have time to go out on the town while they were there. Eleanor was stationed near DC—which was fairly close to Langley Air Force Base, where Missy was stationed—but it was hard to find the time to catch up when they were working all the time and exhausted on their days off. Flying every day took its toll.

Then she realized she hadn't been nearly as nosy as Eleanor had been. "So who made you do the walk of shame?"

Eleanor gave her a cat-who-ate-the-cream smile. "Have you seen that Typhoon with the traditional camo paint job?"

"No way! That's the most beautiful aircraft on the field. I even asked Conrad if he'd find out if the pilot was single."

"I bet he loved that! Well, he is. At least, I assume he is." She frowned for a split second.

Missy wanted to reassure her, but experience had told her that there was a certain type of pilot who thought they could have every woman who had a pulse. Her heart lurched. Conrad was one of them, wasn't he?

"You want to go out tomorrow tonight?" Eleanor asked.

Missy looked at the time on her phone. "You mean tonight?"

"Shit. Yes, I do. Today will be a struggle with so little sleep. But I'm a fierce napper, and we should be back from our mission around twenty hundred hours. Which is way before the festivities kick off in Vegas. Have I ever taken you to Bipartisan Measures?"

"Is that a show?" Missy was confused.

"No, it's a bar. I had my first sexual encounter in the one in DC." She cocked her head. "And one of my most recent."

Missy gave a shocked laugh. "How do you do these things and never get caught?"

"I don't do these things. Well, I guess I did...but..." Her voice trailed off, and her expression grew serious.

"What's the matter?" Missy leaned forward on the bed. Eleanor looked worried. She'd never, ever seen her look worried—about anything.

Eleanor seemed to force a smile on her face. "Well, he has a British accent, so you know, all bets were off." The smile became more natural.

Missy leaned back again and fanned herself with her hand. "Be still my beating heart."

"I know, right? So tonight?"

"Hell yeah. I want to see the scene of the crime. Take photos, hear details..."

Missy's thoughts turned to the mission. "We took out the Aggressor Squadron yesterday," she said, trying not to look too triumphant.

"Not *my* team," Eleanor scoffed.

"I knew it! I knew you'd made the Aggressors!" Missy crowed. She'd guessed that there was no way the Aggressor Squadron would take formation without Eleanor in their ranks. But she never expected her to admit it so readily. Eleanor was right. She did indeed have a true pilot's ego.

"Don't tell anyone. Not even Conrad."

Missy held up three fingers. "Scout's honor."

"Don't forget—I've known you for longer than anyone here. I know you'd only set foot in the Girl Scouts to steal their badges." Eleanor raised her eyebrows meaningfully.

Missy choked on her mouthful of lukewarm coffee. "Okay, okay. Deal. My lips are sealed."

A door closed in the corridor outside, and people started moving around. Missy groaned. "I guess a nap's out of the question now."

"No rest for the wicked," Eleanor said, jumping up from her chair with amazing energy.

"Did you sleep at all?" Missy asked.

"I don't need sleep to be awesome!" she said as she disappeared into the bathroom.

Missy longed to be Eleanor. Just for the day. Endless energy, a hot British guy, and an unshakeable knowledge that she was a winner.

Eleanor also didn't have to fly with Conrad or have to confirm her transfer before he could talk her out of it.

CHAPTER SIX

TechGen-One security consultant Chris Grove stood up from the crouch he and the two mechanics had assumed when Major Missy Malden had started running in their direction. He'd been tracking her since he'd placed a tiny sticker on the back of her sweatshirt in front of the base lodging, and thank God he had. Killing her in front of the mechanics would have been messy.

Not that he hadn't planned out exactly how he'd do it. In the few minutes that he'd known she was on her way, he'd decided that he'd snap her neck and then move a set of aircraft steps next to her plane and leave her at the bottom, with a foot between the rungs. Before anyone would have conclusively determined that it hadn't been an accident, they'd be long gone.

"Come on, let's get this done. We've taken too much time already."

The senior tech guy stood up in the office, too, looking angry. "That wasn't our fault. Gallagher wasn't used to the schematics on the Eurofighter Typhoon. He did fucking well for never having installed the PreCall device on one before."

"I don't care. If he couldn't do it, he should have told the boss he couldn't do it. But he didn't, so that's on you, and him." Jesus. All he was there for was to manage security while they installed the software that General Daniels had been forced to permit. And tweak it a little for Major Daniels and Flight Lieutenant Dex Stone from the Royal Air Force.

Major Daniels had overheard a sensitive conversation between her father and Grove's boss, Mr. Danvers. A very sensitive conversation. One that would expose TGO's illegal dealings, bribes, and kickbacks to government folk, right up to the most important people in the White House.

Danvers didn't like loose ends. Or loose lips. They had to get rid of her—and given that she'd been spending plenty of time with the British pilot as well, it was safest to take them both out. Cauterize the wound before it spread.

The new technology had been designed to enhance an aircraft's maneuverability. It took about two hours to collect data from the pilot's manner of flying, and then it would anticipate the pilot's every move. It was a good product that the TechGen-One CEO had already presold to the Russians. Secretly, of course.

This sneaky software shit wasn't exactly the way Grove was used to operating, though. His style was doing things out in the open. In the military, you had carte blanche to kill people whenever you wanted to, really. No one questioned you; no one minded a bit of torture. That was what he had told himself, anyway. But he'd been wrong—and then dishonorably discharged for behavior unbecoming. He hated the fucking military now, and he loved TGO.

Danvers had taken him off the street, virtually. He had valued the things about him the military hated. He didn't judge Grove; he directed him. And Danvers needed people he could rely on. Loyalty and the ability to do the job, no matter how hard, without question. And Grove got paid handsomely for it.

All this scavenging around aircraft, uploading sketchy software, and stuff like that? It wasn't his scene. A shot straight into the forehead was more his style. But here, on the military base that he swore he would never return to, he got a kick out of targeting these fresh-faced, naïve officers.

The kind of officers who used to look down on him. The kind of officers who'd judged him and had sentenced him at his court-martial. They had no idea what it was like outside the wire. Few officers did.

But Danvers paid him to follow orders, and if that meant babysitting two engineers who could upload something fast—well, it was supposed to be fast—then that was what he would do.

It never ceased to amaze him how easily a mind was focused when a muzzle was applied to a temple. It's funny how quickly the muzzle gets warm, blends to the skin's temperature. He knew how that felt. Every day for a week after being fired from the military, he'd pressed the muzzle of his revolver against his temple, angled slightly backward to ensure a clean shot. But that was before Danvers.

Before TGO.

Now he had a new job, money, and the ability to scratch an itch every time Danvers wanted someone to disappear.

And God, he hoped Danvers wanted to do away with Major Missy Malden. When she'd looked in his eyes, the brief flicker of fear had turned him on. As it always did. But she was not his to take, unless Danvers ordered it.

He was looking down at the engineers working on Major Daniels's aircraft. They knew what to do, how to get in to the airframe's system, without a scratch on a screw or dent on a rivet. That's why they paid them the big bucks.

"Are you done yet?" He could see a trickle of morning light eat through the windows at the top of the hangar above the sliding doors. He felt no fear, though; he would take out anyone who came between him and his mission.

The head engineer rose and nodded at him from beneath the wing of the F-16 that was going to kill Major Daniels. If anything would keep her father in line to deliver the rest of the military to TGO, it would be showing how easily they could get to his family.

So now they were done. Between the three of them, they had killed two pilots, even though the pilots didn't know it yet.

He felt like God. Or maybe Jesus. Maybe Danvers was God. All he cared about was doing his job well so he could keep on getting paid to do what he loved the most—taking lives and making people scared of him. Danvers had given him power over the very people who had tried to wreck his life. He loved his fucking job.

He closed up the engineer's laptop, tucked it under his arm, and climbed down the stairs to the hangar floor. "Let's go," he said to the two engineers. It worried him how nervous the younger one looked. He wasn't used to TGO employees looking nervous about anything they were told to do. He would have to report that back to Danvers.

"Good job, guys," he said with a smile. "You work well under pressure."

The young engineer became more relaxed at his words. He smiled and nodded. They left the hangar through the back door, which led directly onto the taxiway; this meant no early-rising troops would catch them on the flight line.

"So, have you been working for TGO a long time?" he asked the younger of the two engineers.

The older, grizzled engineer gave him a long stare, but he ignored it.

"No, sir," he replied. "Just for a few months."

That was bad news. But I guess they would find out in a few short hours whether or not he would be able to keep his mouth shut. If he was the type just to appreciate his salary and the fact that he got to work on an F-16 today, or if he was the type to report Grove for holding a gun to his head. He hoped it was the former. Only because Langton, the older engineer, was a tough Vietnam vet, not known for taking shit from anyone. He wouldn't put it past him to make a play for him if Grove tried anything with the new guy.

Not that he couldn't take him, as long as he wasn't ambushed, but things were complicated enough without having to deal with the help as well.

Three of them walked back toward Danvers's office, a night's work well done.

CHAPTER SEVEN

Conrad awoke to an empty bed. Confused for a moment, he sat up, alert. *What the hell?* Please, God, don't tell him that had all been a dream. He got up and drew the curtains, wincing at the bright Vegas sun glaring into his room.

No way. She had been here. He could still smell her soap, or shower gel, or something on him. But where was she now? When did she leave? And how the fuck had she done that without him noticing?

He turned around and looked at the room. It was hard to believe every single one of his dreams had come true in this room. This crappy, dull, base lodging room.

She'd left without them being able to talk. Without having figured anything out. And now they wouldn't have an opportunity to do so until that evening. How could he fly with her now, when all he would be able to see was her beautiful naked body that had taken his to such unbelievable heights?

His heart started pumping with excitement. She knew how he felt now. She would stay to complete their tour together, and whatever happened next, they'd be together. She'd given him a huge fucking shock when she'd said that she was going to transfer. He couldn't imagine flying without her, let alone being as successful as they were. Thank God he would now have her close every day.

That had been a close call. After leaving the gym, he'd tried to picture himself flying with another weapons officer. Training them, trying to get them to do everything that Missy could do in her sleep. He smiled to himself. He had a whole lifetime ahead of seeing how she acted in her sleep.

He headed down to the hangar early, hoping to see her there, maybe get a quick chance to talk. Really, he just wanted to see her smile. A smile that contained the knowledge of what they'd shared. An intimate smile he'd never seen before, and really, really wanted to.

The hangar was empty except for Sergeant Cripps. He wiped his hands on a rag and nodded at him. "So where were you last night?" he said, a tinge of humor in his voice.

"What do you mean?" Conrad asked with a frown, his brain whirring from bliss to full alert in a split second.

Cripps motioned toward the cots where Missy and he were supposed to have slept the previous night. Damn. How had he completely forgotten about that? And then he noticed that Missy's was rumpled, as if she'd spent the whole night there, while his was so pristine a pillow chocolate wouldn't have looked out of place.

He mustered his thoughts and presented Cripps with a cocky smile, raising his eyebrows suggestively.

"Enough said, sir." A broad grin broke out on Cripps's face. "Nice. Thank you. That's awesome. Good..." He made to punch him on the upper arm, as if in victory, but Conrad's expression must have stopped him, as his face dropped at the same time as his arm.

"Why is that so awesome?" he asked the sergeant. "I mean, I get that it's awesome for me, but why you?" Suddenly he didn't really want to know the answer.

"You just won me a hundred and sixty bucks." Cripps's smile reemerged.

Conrad was bemused. He really didn't have time for this. He needed to find Missy.

Sergeant Cripps continued. "The rest of the team bet you'd be here to take your night shift watching the aircraft, but I said you'd bail on Major Malden and find some other entertainment. A good omen for the exercises today, right?" Cripps turned back to the aircraft.

All Conrad's excitement and joy evaporated, like they'd never been there.

He was a lieutenant colonel in the U.S. Air Force. A pilot. And the crew chief had put money on the fact that he'd bail on his duty in favor of chasing women. And worse, the rest of the team actually believed that he wouldn't have let Missy down, and now they'd think that they'd been wrong to trust him.

Conrad was pissed, but there was a decent-sized part of

him that was already planning some kind of sexy revenge on Missy for putting him in that position.

As it happened, he didn't catch up with Missy until the morning briefing. He'd waited so long in the hangar hoping she'd turn up and they could speak, that he was the last in to the briefing.

The commander gave him a look, and he pulled an apologetic expression and took the seat behind Missy. He tapped her on the shoulder as he sat.

She half turned and nodded briefly. Same as she always did. His happiness to see her—the back of her, at least—diminished just a fraction. But they were in the classroom with at least twenty other pilots and weapons officers. Obviously they had to appear exactly the same as usual.

Sooner than he imagined possible, he was startled when the commander wrapped up the mission brief. Conrad had not heard one word of it. So much for acting the same as always.

He fell into step next to Missy as they left the building. He opened his mouth to speak, although he wasn't sure what to say, when she interrupted his thoughts.

"I've got a quick meeting. It will only take ten minutes. See you back at the hangar." She didn't wait for a reply, just turned away, lengthened her stride, and disappeared into the admin building.

A slight chill ran through him. Must've been the breeze. Why was nothing feeling like he thought it would be? He wasn't getting any intimate vibes from Missy, and he was now just realizing how much he craved them. Craved *her*, after last night.

He just needed her attention, and it was a totally alien feeling for him. He wanted her to look at him—really look at him. Not the skating, brief eye contact she'd given him. What had happened? He'd got as close to her as physically possible, and now she won't even look at him, let alone talk to him?

Jesus. Had she one-and-done him?

No, that couldn't be it. He had made it clear that he wanted her to stay with him, to fly with him. He must have. Well, he hadn't actually said it, but surely it had been obvious?

He looked around him, taking in the normality of his surroundings. Airmen walking with purpose, civilians holding folders and heading toward meetings, people taking cigarette breaks. It was all so normal, so why did everything feel completely different?

Nothing was right in Missy's head. Clearly she had been avoiding him. She'd run out on him, avoided him, and then red-line confirmed that she wanted a transfer to the schoolhouse in Florida, where she could teach prospective weapons officers.

She tried to stay one step ahead of Conrad all morning. Diving into groups of friends or talking to the crew who maintained her aircraft. She didn't want to see that look in his eyes, the one that she was sure every girl who shared his bed saw. The one that said "you're so beautiful, but I'm not a commitment kind of guy."

She wondered how the other women had taken it. The gymnast, the nurse, the casino hotel receptionist. Maybe they were better than her. Maybe that's what they thought about him too. But not her—Conrad was her weakness, and good weapons officers always understood, and compensated for, their weaknesses.

By the time she got back to the hangar, after confirming her transfer request in the admin block, it was a hive of activity. Aircraft engines were starting on the taxiway, and jets were taking to the air some hundred meters away from them. She breathed a sigh of relief: it was impossible to talk on the flight line—the roar of jet engines rendered it useless to even try, and as soon they had their helmets and comms on, there was no way to talk without somebody else listening in.

It was perfect for her, as it allowed her time to collect her thoughts and figure out what to say to him. Or maybe by avoiding him, or at least avoiding the conversation, he would realize he didn't actually have to tell her that what they'd shared was essentially a one-night stand.

As it happened, their flight was completely normal. They worked together just the same as they always had, beating the enemy and evading missile flares.

Conrad hadn't seemed stressed or anxious to talk to her, so she considered that a win.

They were five minutes away from beginning their descent into Nellis Air Force Base when Missy saw a plume of smoke out of the corner of her eye. She swiveled as far as she could in her seat to see what it had been, but she couldn't. She opened her mouth to ask Conrad to go around again, but before any word managed to escape, she saw a different plume—a dust plume in a clearing below them. A dark shadow emerged through the dust.

It was an aircraft. On the floor of the valley. *What the...?*

"Down there!" she said, leaning forward to poke his shoulder. "It's an aircraft. Down on the ground."

Conrad dipped his left wing to give him a better view of the valley. "Jesus."

"I swear I just saw someone or something move down there," she said.

Conrad waggled his wings in case anyone down there could see them. It would alert them to the fact that they had been located.

Missy opened comms to the control room at Nellis and explained what she had seen. But it wasn't until that they had touched down that she remembered the initial plume of smoke behind her that had made her look down.

As they taxied to the hangar, people ran from the hangar to signal them in. Before the aircraft even came to a halt, Conrad had popped the canopy back.

"Who was it? Who crashed?" Missy shouted at the crew chief as she undid her harness and yanked off her helmet.

"There were two!" Sergeant Cripps shouted back. "Major Daniels and some British dude in a Eurofighter Typhoon."

Oh my God. It was Eleanor. Chills shot through her body, and tears sprung to her eyes. She couldn't move. What had she just seen? Was Eleanor dead? They had to go back. She took a breath. They couldn't go back. Pararescuers were probably already on their way. She took another breath. No this couldn't be happening. "You sure? Are you sure it was her?" She scrambled down from her plane, followed by Conrad.

Cripps looked pale. "Yes, ma'am. I'm sorry. Apparently her father is here too. He's a three-star general."

"Yes, I know that," she said. Anxiety squeezed her internal organs until she could barely breathe. "It can't be true. She's the best pilot here."

Conrad actually looked as if he was about to object to Eleanor being tagged the best pilot, but instead he kept his mouth shut, sensibly, and squeezed her shoulder. "We saw the aircraft, and you said you thought you saw something move. That's a good sign. They'll find her in no time."

Missy took a shaky breath and nodded. She wanted Conrad to wrap his arms around her and hold her. She needed his strength. She couldn't bear the thought of Eleanor being in pain anywhere.

Before Missy could say anything else, two MPs strode up to them. "Colonel. Major. General Daniels wants to see you," the taller of the two said.

Eleanor's father. "Of course. We'll come as soon we've been debriefed," Missy said, untying the bandanna from her head.

"No, ma'am. He wants to see you both immediately."

"Let me just run and get my hat." There was no way she was walking across the base to visit a general without her hat on.

She ran to the changing room and opened her locker. She grabbed a towel and ran it over her head and face to get rid of any helmet grime, tucked her hair behind her ears, and grabbed her hat. She closed the locker door and jumped at the sight of the shorter, stockier MP who was waiting for her behind it. What the hell?

"I was just getting my hat! Did you think I was going to try to escape?" she snorted.

"Escape from what exactly, ma'am?" the MP asked.

"Nothing, I mean..." Suddenly the sweat on her body turned cold and a feeling of danger prickled over her body, a sensation she hadn't felt since she'd been a teenager. She didn't like it.

What the hell is going on?

CHAPTER EIGHT

Conrad was worried about Missy. She hadn't said a word, neither to him nor to the MPs escorting them, since they set off across the flight line to General Daniels's office.

It was obvious that seeing the downed aircraft had shaken her. He wanted to comfort her, to hold her hand or put his arm around her, but he couldn't.

As the MPs knocked, then stepped aside from the general's door, he could feel the tension radiating from her. Why was she so stressed? Was it the fact that there were two pilots missing, or was it to do with last night? Both? He hated not being able to talk to her. He was so used to understanding her perfectly.

Except that wasn't exactly true. In fact, as he began to think more about it, he wondered if he even knew her at all. He had no idea she was considering a transfer. Now that he thought about it, he knew nothing about her. He tried to remember their conversations. Why hadn't she ever told him anything? She was from Montana. No, that was the crew chief. Shit. He didn't even know where she was from. Her accent gave no clue. He tried to visualize

her family. But he didn't even know if she had one. No one
had ever visited her on base. That he knew of. A coldness
seeped into him as he realized that everything he knew
about her only related to how well she helped him do his
job. Had she been right about that? He cared about her
more than he could verbalize, but it suddenly seemed as
if it was a totally self-absorbed caring. He was a complete
dick.

"Colonel. Major," the general snapped, making Conrad
start.

Missy and he remained at attention in front of the large
oak desk. The general was seated, but at his right shoulder
was a civilian Conrad recognized as the guy in charge of
TechGen-One—the contractor who was running Red Flag
that year.

"This isn't the time for silence," the general said.

How could the general possibly not realize that they
were not going to talk to him while they were standing at
attention? Was he confused? Was he . . . ?

"My daughter is missing."

Conrad was about to open his mouth and ask for permission to stand ease, when Missy spoke.

"I know, sir." Her voice trembled.

Conrad was astonished but suddenly had no idea what
was going on. Why would the general think that they
were being silent to keep things from him? After all,
Missy had only seen the outline of the plane. They were
just unfortunate witnesses. To something horrible.

"I've been told that you both spent the night in the hangar last night," the general said.

Wait, what?

"I need to know what you saw. Did anyone touch her plane?"

Conrad felt dread clawing up his spine. This was not good. Why did the general automatically assume someone had done something to his daughter's aircraft? Conrad had been involved with aircraft investigations before, and criminal action was not normally the first assumption. Unless the general, and this contractor, knew something that no one else knew. Missy had seen that aircraft on the floor of the valley less than an hour previously. Assuming they had no contact with either pilot, the automatic assumption should be some kind of pilot error, especially when two aircraft were involved. Yet the general had gone directly to sabotage, without passing go, without collecting $200.

Something wasn't right.

"No, sir, we didn't see anything." At least that was the truth. The general didn't even look at him when he spoke.

General Daniels kept Missy firmly pinned in his gaze. "If you didn't see anything, maybe you did something yourself? Or maybe you saw the lieutenant colonel here do something."

Conrad froze. The shit show just got real. He was accusing them of espionage, treason, murder, sabotage. He wanted to grab Missy's hand and tell her to stop talking.

"No, absolutely not! How could you possibly...?" Her voice trailed off, which to Conrad's untrained ear, made her sound guilty, or confused, or scared. Not a good look to a general on the warpath.

He intervened as best he could. "Missy and your daughter are friends. Neither of us would ever damage somebody else's aircraft. How could you possibly already know it wasn't an accident?"

"Because there's no other explanation," he shouted. "They were both the best pilots in their squadrons."

Conrad wasn't going to take the general's raised voice sitting down. "For the want of a lock, the country was lost. Right, sir? A simple lock on the hangar door would have prevented any suspicion of sabotage."

"My daughter could be dead and you're lecturing me about locks?" the general spluttered, his face turning red. Was he about to have a heart attack?

"Wait," Missy said. "There was someone else in her hangar yesterday morning. Some civilians. I could point them out if you like. They even had a golf cart in there. But Eleanor told me she'd already spoken to you about it."

The general's demeanor changed instantly. He looked shocked. Scared even. Didn't he know that TGO had contractors in and around the hangars?

"Eleanor told you about our conversation?" he asked quietly, eyes on his desk, almost wincing.

"Of course she did. We're friends, and we were both worried about possible damage."

The general's eyes closed as if he were in deep pain. The contractor guy—what was his name? Danvers—placed his hand gently on General Daniels's shoulder. It could have been a gesture of solidarity, but somehow it didn't seem like that to Conrad. Something weird was going on here, and somehow he and Missy were caught up in it.

"You two will be held under house arrest in barracks until we get to the bottom of this." The general swiveled in his seat and didn't look as the two MPs—apparently with their ears to the door—came in and led them out.

What the fuck was going on? Nineteen years in the air force and nothing like this had ever happened to him before. Conrad hadn't even ever heard of anything like this happening to anyone.

He tried to catch Missy's attention, but her eyes were on the ground. What was she thinking? He knew what she was thinking. Like him, she was realizing that if they came clean, they would be fired, and if they didn't, they could go to jail anyway. Unless she really did know something.

He managed to stroke his thumb over her hand as they were led away. She raised her eyes to his and frowned.

CHAPTER NINE

The general's hands clenched in his lap.

"It's okay. I'll have someone deal with this," Danvers said.

"You've dealt with enough," the general ground out through clenched teeth. He couldn't believe this was happening to him.

He couldn't believe that after a career of following the laws and serving his country, just one occasion of bending the rules could lead to this. He was neck deep in a shit show and he couldn't see a way out. And now TechGen-One had Eleanor in their sights. If she was still alive. Emotion choked him, and he had to concentrate to breathe.

"I told you not to allow your daughter to fly at Red Flag. I knew it would be a needless complication. I told you that, didn't I?" Danvers said, slowly walking to the front of his desk, picking up things from his desk and looking at them, as if he owned them. Owned him.

He did.

"She deserved it. She worked hard for this," he said. It

was true she was the best, most instinctive pilot he'd ever seen fly. But his attempt to maybe make her not hate him as much had all but signed her death warrant.

"Well, I think it's clear now who the boss of Red Flag is. You do what I say or suffer the consequences. You can't touch me without ruining yourself. If you decide to talk, I will take you down with me. There's nothing noble about a maximum-security prison. And don't think for a moment I will be joining you. My support network goes right up to the West Wing. Does yours?"

Daniels couldn't believe that he had let himself get caught in the crosshairs of this monster. He thought he was going to be seen as a hero when a business associate offered to pay the operational costs of Red Flag. Then he'd stupidly accepted some company shares and an interest-free loan to pay for a large, secure beach house. And at no point had he thought that it was too good to be true. He had served his country for thirty years; he deserved it. He deserved the good luck, the recognition, the vacations, share portfolio, and the villa by the sea.

And it wasn't until three weeks previously, when he had been asked to secretly allow modifications on certain aircraft, that he realized he could not get out of the noose that Danvers and TechGen-One had around his neck. He was in too deep.

"You see what you've done? Your daughter told Missy about your conversation. She is now a loose end, like Eleanor was. You've left me with another mess to take care of. You want to be careful, General, because if you cause too many problems, you, too, will be a loose end."

He didn't reply.

"I suggest you plan on returning to the Pentagon. And leave me here to tidy up."

The general knew it wasn't a suggestion. And he knew that by leaving, he would be casting suspicion on himself. It was Danvers's way of showing him the slippery slope he was teetering at the top of right now.

CHAPTER TEN

Missy had no idea what had happened to her life. One second she'd been getting closure before transferring, and the next moment she was getting arrested for something she couldn't prove she didn't do without giving up both her and Conrad's careers. What sweet hell was this?

They were both frog-marched over to the old barracks building and handed over to two TGO men, who wore polo shirts and ostentatious sidearms.

The building had peeling paint—lead paint? she wondered—and smelled like a hundred young airmen had left their dirty laundry there for ten years. The men's bathroom also added an acrid note to the heady bouquet even with its door shut.

Conrad was separated from her as they walked through the building. She kind of hoped he'd be housed closer to the men's restroom than she was.

She was 100 percent convinced that the men in the hangar, the accidents today, and the fact that she'd been sent to the slammer as soon as she mentioned the conversation Eleanor had had with her father were all connected along a line that had TGO running straight through it.

She'd tried not to engage Conrad on their short walk there. She didn't want him thinking he had to be the hero to save her or to sacrifice his career to be her alibi. In fact, he couldn't be her alibi since she left without him noticing. She shrugged as she sat on the small cot—the only furniture in the room. She guessed that was the night for her. The sun was setting, and clearly no one was coming to say, "Oops—we made a mistake."

Closing her eyes, she allowed herself a moment to remember the previous night. Conrad had touched her. Touched something primal, something so deep inside that it scared her. She had to get away from him. If their night together had taught her nothing else, it was that she had to escape him and his spell over her. She was in too deep and couldn't bear the thought of him talking about a waitress he'd bedded, or a nurse, or a fucking gymnast. No. Way. That was done.

She shrugged to herself and lay down on top of the dark green blanket that had been folded on the cot. She was either going to jail, transferring to MacDill, or...yeah, she didn't have any other options. It wasn't as if she could go crash with her parents, because (A) she doubted they had anywhere for her to crash, and (B) she had no idea where they were—or even if they were still alive. She paused for a second, probing her heart for feelings about that, but found none.

There was a knock at the door. She felt stupid saying "come in" since she couldn't open the door herself, nor was she at liberty to say who could come in or not. A key rattled in the lock and it swung open to reveal a senior airman holding two bags of what looked like fast food. A TGO employee stood behind him.

"Sergeant Cripps sent me here with food for you and Colonel Conrad, ma'am, but it seems as if they've already released Colonel Conrad. I guess you can have both of these."

"Thank you," she said, but her mind was processing the fact that they'd let him go. So the focus was really just on her. What had Conrad said to them that made them release him? Had he just left her there?

The airman backed away and the TGO guy sneered at her with his hand threateningly on his sidearm. What a douche. She could take him so easily if she wanted. Hell. She could have taken him before she joined the air force. She winked at him, and he slammed the door, but not before she clocked the look of annoyed confusion on his face.

Considering herself a weird POW, she decided to eat everything on offer, in case it was a while before she was fed again. She ate a burger and fries and some kind of fruit pie. She was so full by then that the thought of eating Conrad's dinner, too, made her feel ill. She was about to stuff the wrappers back in the paper bag when she saw grease-stained handwriting on the inside. She ripped the bag open.

I'll come for you.

She rolled her eyes. Dramatic much? Conrad watched too many movies. But she couldn't deny that her heart beat just a little faster at the thought of being rescued by him. Damn. Maybe *she'd* watched too many movies.

If she was going to be here all night, she may as well get comfortable. She banged on the door and demanded a bathroom break—although it being an old building, it was barely more than a latrine. Still the sink had running water and she was able to clean herself up after the afternoon flying in the heat of the desert. She walked barefoot back to her room, holding her boots and ignoring the push the TGO guy gave her when he opened the door to her room.

"You better behave tonight," he said, his breath floating on the already stale air.

"Or what?" she said, because she couldn't help herself.

"We've been authorized to use force." He grinned. "And I'm looking forward to it."

She slammed her foot on the floor as if she were reaching for him, and he jumped back, immediately furious that he'd shown his fear.

Missy winked at him again, and again, he slammed the door and locked it.

She was having flashbacks to her teenage years, when she was all piercings and bad attitude. In fact, now that she thought about it, she felt as if she was regressing to her behavior back then. When she was scared, and fight or flight kicked in, she never, ever took flight. She always stopped and fought. Always won, until everyone in the neighborhood was scared of her, except her parents. They floated off, leaving her alone in the house for days, and then would come back stoned. But they'd been the only constant in her life, and it had taken her years to leave them behind. She had no idea where they were now. And she didn't care.

She took off her uniform pants and shirt and lay on the cot, staring at the ceiling. She could feel strains of the old Missy returning. For years now she'd been the good Missy. The totally by-the-book, squared-away Missy. The top-of-the-class Missy. No one here knew her as the Missy-from-a-bad-home, or the truant Missy, or the didn't-graduate-high-school-the-first-time Missy.

Until today, she had forgotten that Missy. That Missy had disappeared the day the judge forced her into boot camp. But now she remembered who she really was. If she wanted to keep her career, she had to be the good Missy on the outside but keep the old, wary, suspicious Missy on the inside.

The good Missy. She allowed herself to succumb to the tiredness that made her eyes heavy and drifted away into an uncertain future.

A knocking awoke her. She was alert and upright immediately. The room was still dark and undisturbed. She looked around and stifled a gasp when she saw a face at the window. Damn him. It was Conrad.

She shook her head. He mimed at her to open the window. *The windows opened?* She undid the latch and the window swung out. Jesus. She could have gone back to her own room to shower and then sneaked back in again.

"Yeah, the barracks weren't designed to be secure," Conrad said with a shrug and a satisfied grin on his face.

"What are you doing here? What time is it?"

"Oh-two-hundred, give or take. I've come to provide you with a little less solitary confinement and a little more information. Are you coming? This place isn't secure, but someone's going to find me eventually standing here."

She hesitated for a second. But unless they shot her, she couldn't figure anything else going worse for her than they already were. "Let me get dressed."

"There's no time. Besides, I've seen more of you at PT." He opened his mouth again after a pause, and then closed it. She knew he was going to make some reference to the previous night but had decided against it. It was the right decision.

"Come on, come on. Seriously, the guy who patrols here has just gone inside to get a cup of coffee." He stood back from the window and beckoned her. "Hurry."

"I need my boots." She turned back into the room.

"Jesus, when did you get this bad at obeying orders? Just climb the fuck out of the window."

She slithered out headfirst. He caught her and shifted her onto his back.

"Put me down," she hissed.

"In a minute," he replied, looking around them, and then ran across the road and across the athletics track. His shoulder dug into her stomach, and she felt every mouthful of her fast-food dinner swirl angrily around.

"Conrad! Put me..."

He lowered her carefully onto a swing at the children's playground. She blew her hair out of her face and watched as he took the swing next to hers. "You take me to all the nicest places," she said.

"But at least I bring beer." He grabbed two bottles from a cooler he'd obviously stashed there earlier.

She clinked the neck with his. "Well, then, all is forgiven."

There was a moment of silence as they watched the old barracks building. One office had a light on, but the rest were dark. She could see one person patrolling the circumference. "I wonder if there are any other prisoners," she said.

"Nope. It's only you. Okay. This is what I've heard so far. TGO has found the wreckage of both aircraft..."

"Wait a minute. Why aren't the pararescuers out looking for them?" That was the deal every service member made—not just U.S. service members, but all allied military. That if something happened to them, the pararescuers would go get them. They were the best in the world.

"Apparently Eleanor's father gave away the house when TGO brought their money to Red Flag. They were allowed complete operational control—which they only took after the accident." Conrad took another swig of beer. "This whole thing smells off to me, and I don't like that you're in the middle of it."

"You and me both," she said. "After we saw that TGO golf cart come out of the hangar, I recognized the man who was on it. He approached me when I was..." She paused. "Coming to lodging to pick you up to go to the hangar. I pretended I didn't know him, but he followed me into the hotel and up to your floor."

"What? Why didn't you say something?" Conrad stopped swinging and turned to her.

"You didn't give me much chance." She raised her eyebrows meaningfully. "And in the morning, it didn't seem to matter that much."

"What did you do in the morning? I woke and you'd already gone."

She looked away from him and started to swing. "I went to the hangar to mess up our beds, so it'd look like we'd been there all night. But when I got there, I figured I'd play a joke and leave your cot alone so that you'd have to do some quick thinking when you came in. It was supposed to be funny." She paused again. "I got there just before dawn, and the hangar was really dark, but I swear I felt that someone was there. You know, when you feel the air disturbed around you?"

"You sure you weren't feeling a disturbance in the Force?" he quipped.

She ignored him and took another gulp of the cold beer.

Damn, she would probably need to pee again when she got back to her room.

Conrad spoke again. "Do you think someone was there? In the hangar? It could have been someone working on Eleanor's F-16. Why didn't you say something?"

"Are you kidding? They're accusing me of sabotage, and I blame it on an invisible person I thought may have been in the hangar? Talk about seeming obviously guilty of something. And then how exactly do I explain why I only came into the hangar just before sunrise? Do you want to lose your job?"

He turned his swing around and grabbed the chain on hers. "I don't want to lose *you* to this craziness. Something is going down here, and you seem to have been set up as the scapegoat. All I have to do is come clean, which I'm going to do in the morning. I'll tell Colonel Cameron what happened—"

"Nope. That wouldn't even work. His first question before firing us would be 'and were you with her all night?' and you'd have to say no. And then you'd have to admit that you didn't know what time I left your room or what I did when I left. The only thing you'll gain from that is having to beg TGO for a job." She didn't want to admit it, but a warmth spread through her at the thought that he'd put his whole career on the line for her.

"Firstly, I'd never ask TGO for a job. Nothing about that company feels good. But I am going to see Colonel Cameron. I trust him—I've known him for years, and he knows me. We were in the same squadron before he moved here to run Red Flag."

She shook her head. "I don't see any of this ending well for us."

"I promise I'll provide conjugal visits if you end up in the slammer," he said.

"You'll provide them? Like, you'll send someone? Do I get to pick...?"

He grabbed her chin and made her face him. "No one gets to touch you except me. Not on my watch." He hesitated after he said the words, and she wondered if he realized how cheesy-movie he sounded.

She tried not to laugh, and his eyes narrowed at her effort. In less than a second his lips were on hers. Rampant desire flooded her body as his tongue thrust into her mouth, dominating her. Damn.

She dropped her beer bottle into the sawdust at her feet and kissed him back, matching him touch for touch, stroke for stroke. Without skipping a beat, he knelt in front of her and put his hands around her back to stop her from swinging away from him.

He angled his head, almost punishing her mouth with a ferocity that set her on fire. She grabbed his head and pulled him even closer, reveling in the burst of desire that turned her thoughts to mush.

His fingers grasped the bottom of her T-shirt and yanked it over her head. Her nipples hardened at the contact with the cool air.

"Jesus, you're beautiful in moonlight," he whispered as his lips descended to her breasts. He tongued each nipple, sending spirals of excitement through her body, and then bit them, making her back arch and her head tip back in surrender.

He pulled at one nipple as his hands dragged her underwear shorts down and off.

God help her; she was naked, on a swing, on Nellis Air Force Base. And she was supposed to be under house arrest. The frisson of terror and excitement set her nerve endings on fire. She felt every waft of breeze on her skin as if it were someone's fingers; every breath she took felt as if she were inhaling freedom and inhibition.

Conrad picked her up off the swing—a feat of strength that surprised her—strode across the playground with her in his arms, and carefully put her down on the picnic table.

Missy stretched across the hard, rough surface of the wood, relishing in the indiscretion and blatant offering of herself to him. She raised herself onto her elbows and held his gaze. This was so different from the night before. She was so different. "See something you like?"

His eyes widened as she deliberately let her legs fall open, but only for a second.

"I don't know," he said, trailing his fingers gently down from her cleavage to her stomach. One finger lightly touched her between her legs, before scooting away again, to make patterns on her stomach.

She bit back a groan. She was so wet. With her foot, she traced his dick through his jeans. He froze as his fingers were about to pluck at one of her nipples. And then he rolled it between his fingertips and squeezed it. A line of electricity buzzed between her breast and her clitoris. She could feel blood pumping up and down it.

"If you don't touch me, I'm going to have to touch myself, Conrad. Don't make yourself obsolete." It would have sounded more convincing if her voice hadn't been so low and whispery with need.

His hands snatched away from her. "Really? You'll touch yourself?" he said.

"If you won't..."

He swiveled her around so that she was crossways on the table, instead of lengthways. She sat up, dizzy with need.

He sat between her legs on one of the benches and growled, "Show me."

Jesus. What was happening here? Missy had a brief flashback to a week ago, when they only ever saw each other in uniform and they only talked shop. Suddenly their professional relationship seemed to have happened years ago.

She sat up straight, planting her feet on either side of him. If he wanted a show, he'd get a show.

Slowly, she tucked her hair behind her ears and trailed her fingers down from her hair to her breasts. Her nipples puckered again under her touch, and she felt more liquid pool between her legs.

Conrad's breath was heavy, and he was practically vibrating. His hands slipped around her ankles and then up to push her knees farther apart.

Her hands moved down her stomach, and then slowly along her thighs to her knees, and then back up.

His hands tightened on her legs as she stroked her inner thigh. Her insides clenched with the intensity of his stare as she extended a finger, dragged it through her wetness, and then slid it to her clit. The pressure was exquisite; the experience of Conrad watching her in this most intimate performance heightened every sense. She stroked her clit slowly and firmly, rocking her pelvis as she did.

"Jesus," he whispered.

She stopped touching herself, desperately wanting him to make her orgasm, and placed her finger on his lips. He opened his mouth immediately and sucked in her finger. He groaned and closed his eyes as he tasted her. His mouth was hot.

Her heart was thumping so hard in her chest, she was sure it was visible through her skin.

He put a hand between her breasts and pushed her back down on the table. Instantly his tongue was on her, licking, probing, and then flicking at her clit.

Her orgasm was ready to break hard. She watched Conrad's head between her legs and couldn't hold back. Her moans echoed around them. In a second he was kneeling on the table next to her, his hand firmly over her mouth to keep her quiet. His tongue returned to her clit, stoking her orgasm front and center. She tensed the second it hit and rocked against his mouth as he took her flying.

For some reason, his hand over her mouth leant a frisson of naughtiness to the already-hot situation. What was wrong with her? What had happened to the demure Missy of last week? Last month?

She didn't care. She sat up and pressed her hand against his hard dick. "I guess I should go back to my room, huh?" she teased.

"Of course," he growled, trying obviously to even out his breathing.

"Unless..." She unzipped his jeans and pushed them over his hips to the ground. "Unless you have a few seconds to spare?" she asked, eyes open wide with mock innocence.

"Who are you, and what have you done with Missy?" he asked, spinning her around and bending her over the table.

"Do you mind?" She looked over her shoulder.

"I don't know what I'm feel..." he began.

Missy didn't wait to hear the answer. Maybe she was scared to. She took his dick into her hand and placed it right at her entrance, flexing herself against him.

"Wait. Give me a moment," he ground out. He grabbed his discarded jeans and pulled a condom out of his pocket. Missy grabbed it from him and opened it gently with her teeth, her gaze not leaving his. She took it out of the packet and placed it on the tip of his dick. His eyes narrowed and his chest heaved as if he'd just ran a marathon.

She bent her head and rolled it on with her mouth. Slowly, inch by inch. He jerked in her mouth.

"Fuck," he said, one hand on her head as she came back up.

Still holding him in her hand, she placed him right where she wanted him the most.

In one slow stroke, he filled her entirely.

A heaviness settled along her limbs as he moved inside her. She bent over the table, allowing her erect nipples to be scraped by the rough surface. The duel sensation of being filled and abraded sent tremors through her.

Conrad slipped his hand around her and stroked her clit in time with his thrusts. The trifecta of desire threw her over the edge, this time a sharper, faster, more intense orgasm. It hit her without warning, and as she muffled her cries with her hand, she felt him spasm inside her. His hands took her hips and rocked her against him.

Neither of them said a word.

As the afterglow left her, she suddenly felt exposed and a little awkward. She stood, and he wrapped his arms around her, holding her tight against him, nuzzling her neck.

After a couple of minutes, he broke his silence with the words she dreaded. "We need to talk about this."

Really? Now?

"No. I should go back. That can be a conversation for another day." She disengaged from him and walked as nonchalantly as possible back to her clothes. She put them on and then picked up her beer bottle and took a drink, as casual as possible.

By the time she'd turned around, Conrad had re-arranged himself and pulled his jeans back on.

"We need to strategize about getting you out of this and back to the squadron," he said. "This is ridiculous. We're the best team up there. Keeping you here is...is damaging our country's security." His voice was getting louder.

She put a hand on his arm. "No, it isn't. There are plenty of people as good as we are, and you'll find someone great to fly with." She smiled at him. "I'm putting you in charge of finding someone new and protecting the country with your awesome piloting stuff."

"What are you talking about? This fuckery will be sorted out soon, and we'll be back to normal." He looked at the barracks. "I'm getting you a JAG first thing, get this done and dusted."

She had a feeling that getting a judge advocate general—a military lawyer—might spring her, but definitely wouldn't put her back on flight duty.

"Conrad, I told you. I'm leaving. After Red Flag, I go home, pack my things, and move to MacDill Air Force Base in Florida. It's already done. I should have orders tomorrow, assuming I'm not arrested on high treason."

"What?" he said between clenched teeth.

"I told you last night that I'd put in for a transfer. This

morning they told me that my old commander is there and jumped at the chance to have me as an instructor."

"But I thought..."

Heat rose in her—but a totally different kind of heat now. "You thought you'd fucked that idea right out of me? Is that it?" she said, barely managing to keep her voice down.

His face registered shock, but also an admission.

"Seriously? You thought that if you took me to bed, you'd get me to stay?" Her hand flew to her belly, where a storm of betrayal and distress was brewing. "It's like I don't even know you. No, you know what? I do know you. I've heard about all the women you fuck and your laser focus on your career. It was me who was stupid enough to believe for a second that you'd be concerned about my career, about my future, about what I want. But now I know for absolute sure who you are."

She turned and ran. Over the grass and the track, to the foot of her window. She didn't look back and disappeared as fast as she could.

In the dark of her room, she stood for a moment, trying to catch her breath. Everything was different now. Everything was wrong. She had no one. How could she have thought for a second that he'd be looking out for her and not just himself? He hadn't changed at all. She could see that now. And she was seven kinds of stupid for expecting him to be different with her.

Fighting back a wave of emotion that threatened tears,

she lay back on her bed and counted missiles. Two in each bay, four in each aircraft, twenty in each hangar, two hundred in the lockup. Her breathing steadied, and her heart rate slowed. She took a couple of deep breaths and closed her eyes.

She had to get out of this mess by herself.

CHAPTER ELEVEN

Conrad hadn't slept worth a shit. His eyes were gritty and his temper was far from even keel. He just wanted someone to look at him wrong so he could take out his frustration physically. He was consumed with too many emotions to name. Not that he truly understood any emotion that wasn't hair-raising fear, anger, or anxiety.

What he wouldn't give to dial the clock back forty-eight hours. Everything was fucked to hell now. Missy had totally bought the endless women he made up. Of course, he only started lying about the women to make excuses for why he never went to social events with her. Then they'd joked about the number of women he pretended he'd slept with, and then it became his schtick. Stupid, stupid move. And how did you ever tell anyone that you'd been lying to them for two years?

He left his room and went to the lobby. There were loads of people in civvies, milling around, talking in low voices.

He saw a pilot he'd been on patrolling sorties with on the Korean peninsula. "Hey. What's going on?"

The Animal—as he was always known—shook his hand. Unusually for him, he looked somber. "I'm arranging a..." He paused to search for the right word.

"Posse," another pilot suggested.

"Yeah, I'm organizing a posse to go out and look for Eleanor and Dex. You heard, right? Of course you did. We decided last night—"

"In the bar," the other pilot added.

"Look, who's telling this story, man?" The Animal was an American-raised Korean national who was a legend at Red Flag, He was the guy who put everything on the line every time he took off and left nothing on the field when he landed.

The pilot grinned and held up both hands. His cell phone rang as soon as he did, and he took the call.

The Animal nodded. "Okay, we were in the bar, but where else do I get my great ideas?"

"It's a mystery to us all," Conrad replied with a patience he definitely wasn't feeling.

"We don't trust TGO. Too many people have too many stories about various fuck-ups they've had downrange. You know? Ones that don't make the official reports."

Really? So maybe Missy and he were right to think that this all revolved around TGO.

"I hadn't heard that," he said, leaning against one of the armchairs.

"It seems as if you have to be directly involved to know what happened, because as I said, none of the incidents make it to the reports." The Animal was tapping his fingers against his leg and was clearly amped up. "I hear that TGO has deep connections to your government. Like entrenched for many years."

"I hope you're not saying my government is corrupt?" Conrad frowned.

"No more than mine. But power and money corrupt individuals. And that's where the shit hits the fan. Anyway, none of us feels real comfortable leaving Eleanor and Dex's rescue to TGO. You want in?"

"Sure I do. But the base is on lockdown."

"I think I have someone who can help me with that," he said. "Someone on the inside."

"Okay, I'll help if I can, but I can't come with you. My weapons officer—Major Malden—is under house arrest, and I feel like they're trying to pin the accident on her."

The Animal's eyebrows rose. "Dude, if you think TGO has her in their sights, I'd keep a real close eye on her." He put his hand on Conrad's arm. "Seriously. I'd give anything to be able to pin this shit storm on them. They deal with my government, too, and it's only a matter of time before they fuck up over there too. And I don't want to see that. The stakes are too damn high in my neck of the woods."

"I'll let you know if I find anything. Thanks, brother."

They shook hands. As Conrad left, he heard the other pilot say that he'd rented a van from Hertz. God only knew what exactly they were planning. He had a flash image of a Mad Max–style convoy of multinational forces, storming the desert to find their missing troops. It brought a smile to his face, and he would have given nearly anything to be a part of it.

But he wasn't going to leave Missy alone, even if she begged him to. Even if she was pissed off to hell with him. He had this unnerving feeling that if he walked away, everyone else would turn a blind eye. And he wasn't about to let that happen.

He marched over to Colonel Cameron's office, ready to confess his sins and explain what he thought TGO was up to. To see if Cameron would step up and help Missy.

Only then could he try to figure out a way to keep her in his life. If she'd have him. And for the life of him he couldn't think of a good reason why she should. He knew knee-trembling, earth-shattering sex wouldn't be enough to make her love him. He didn't even really want to think about what a prick he'd been to her.

A good officer would have at least asked what her career goals were and ensured that she was put in a position where she would get the relevant experience to achieve them. He hadn't. Hell, he knew more about the Animal than he did his own weapons officer. He'd never asked her anything about herself. He wondered why. No, he didn't wonder why. He knew why. He was just scared to acknowledge it.

God only knew how he could fix all this, but he did know that the key to everything was getting her away from TGO and out of house arrest.

CHAPTER TWELVE

Casey Jacobs sat on an uncomfortable plastic chair outside the command center, constantly swiping the TGO screen saver on her phone to check it was still on. She dialed her office number. Yup. Her phone was working. So why wasn't anyone calling her back?

She was TechGen-One's vice president of military marketing, which meant something bad was going on if no one was returning her calls.

Briefly she slumped, holding her head in her hands, trying not to give in to the paralyzing feeling that her company was responsible for the missing pilots in the Nevada desert.

When she'd left the military, she'd been an MC-130J pilot at the top of her game. But with the niggling suspicion that her career had already reached its apex, she'd been receptive when a recruiter contacted her about working for TechGen-One. They offered to double her wage as a lieutenant colonel in the air force—which was already a lot. She'd been assured that she'd still be serving her country, but just not in uniform and without the regulations and constraints that the military put on its service people.

So, she'd resigned her commission and accepted a job with the well-regarded military contractor. All her friends were jealous, and Casey was on cloud nine on her first day in their state-of-the-art offices in Washington, DC.

Except after the lunch she'd had with Mr. Danvers and the other VPs, she'd been taken to legal, shut in a room, and been given a nondisclosure agreement to sign. It wasn't just any confidentiality contract. It took her seven and a half hours to read, initial, and sign every pertinent page. It covered company patents, products, clients, advancements and services, memos, reports, and anything discussed by TGO employees.

It had felt overwhelming when she'd seen the stack of papers. And then she felt pride that they trusted her with their business—which they clearly took so seriously—and that she'd finally landed a position where she could take her career as far as she wanted.

Now, however, as she waited for her call back, doubt prickled her thoughts. Had she signed all those pieces of paper so she couldn't talk to anyone about product failures?

She straightened her spine and tried to find the confidence in TGO she'd had before Red Flag. She could do this.

She swiped her phone again. Why wasn't Malcom calling her back? He was the closest thing to a friend she'd had at the company. He'd been assigned as her buddy her first week there to show her around the campus, and they'd been tight ever since.

The thought of the rambling voice mail she'd left him made her wince. But she was sure he'd forgive her moment of panic.

Casey was able to apply her knowledge as a pilot to help the research and development department fine-tune their concept for new products. The software they were testing here at Red Flag had gone through a number of iterations before she joined the company, and like the good employee she was, she'd taken all the files home and read up on the notes from inception to prototype in her spare time. She liked to be on top of her game, and extracurricular work never fazed her.

PreCall had been designed to give allied pilots a split-second advantage over their enemies. It was designed to learn a pilot's unique way of flying. To detect shifts in physical movement and to predict what the pilot would do in any given situation. All it took was a few hours on an exercise, and the device could align to a pilot's way of flying, his or her intentions, and trigger the aircraft systems a fraction of a second before the pilot reacted to a situation.

Gaining just that extra second in reflex time would make a world of difference in combat. As long as only your side had the technology.

But the static over the radio that she'd heard in the control room and the sudden uncontrollability of the aircraft that the pilots had called in just before the accident were exactly the same as the problems they'd had with the prototype a year previously. She thought they'd fixed that. All she could think was that they'd either installed an earlier model of PreCall on the aircraft accidentally, or the newer version was reverting to old issues.

Either way, she needed answers. She was not going to sell these to the U.S. military if they had problems. Whatever the pressure.

She swiped her phone again—yes, she still had perfect reception—and headed outside to thaw the air-conditioned chill out of her bones.

The desert air should have been oppressive, but instead it relaxed her. She was all about the sun on her skin. She shrugged off her business jacket and stood for second, face to the sun, in her high-necked, sleeveless sweater and her black jeans.

She put on her sunglasses and looked around. It was definitely not business as usual. After the crashes, any remaining exercises had been canceled. Airmen stood around in huddles, all obviously devastated about the loss of the two pilots. She swallowed hard. She'd never lost a crew member in her whole military career, and the fact that she'd met Major Eleanor Daniels just before the accident hit her hard.

Her phone suddenly rang, and she juggled it in surprise. It was Malcolm. *Thank God.*

"Hey, babe," he said.

How could he sound so unconcerned? "Did you get my message? We've lost two aircraft in what looks like—"

"Casey," he said, his voice sharp in response. "Whatever you're about to say, can it until you get back to the office."

She couldn't believe he wasn't as devastated as she was. "I recognize the issue. I was in the control room as the news came in. There was static, and then—"

"I'm warning you, Casey. Drop it. Those confidentiality papers you signed when you started working? They will result in you losing everything. When TGO senses disloyalty, they're...resolute in their response. And it's not a good response, trust me." He suddenly sounded a little shaky.

She said nothing, just looked at the photo of Malcolm on her phone. "You've got to be kidding. I won't let them get away with it, if it is our product that—"

"Jesus, Casey. I wouldn't kid about something like this. You think you're still working for the military, but you're not. Simmer down, have a drink, and forget this conversation. Think about what I'm saying." His voice sounded as if a certain weight was put behind his words. She paused. Could they be monitoring her calls? Maybe everyone's calls? Or was Malcolm just paranoid?

Well, shit. Now she was paranoid too. She put on a light tone. "Sure. You're right. It's just the heat getting to me. I'll get some water and lie down. Al Chile's when I get home?"

He sighed with what sounded like relief. "Sure. Guac's on me."

She forced a laugh. "Sounds good."

He hung up. She shoved the phone in her skirt's side pocket and took a breath. What just happened? What was she going to—

Her phone beeped. It was an email from Malcolm. Hurriedly she opened it, wondering if he was explaining on email something he couldn't say over the phone. But he hadn't written anything except "Wilcom = TGO." He'd attached a link to the *Connecticut Daily News*.

She clicked on it.

Guilty Contractor Kills Self, Leaves Note

Newport, CT: June 26, 2008. James Turner, 46, was found hanged at his home in Newport, Connecticut, yesterday by his landlord.

Turner, who had worked as a data analyst for the military contractor Wilcom, lost a $50-million lawsuit against the company last January and had allegedly been unable to pay his rent for several months. Upon discovering the body, his landlord called 911.

In 2007, Wilcom claimed that Turner had leaked proprietary information to an online reporter and sued him for breach of contract. The information has never been published, and the police have been unable to find the recipient of the leaked documents. Nevertheless, Turner admitted to being a whistleblower, but according to the judge, it wasn't enough to relieve him of his duties under the contract he had signed with Wilcom.

Funeral arrangements have yet to be made.

Casey's breath became shaky as she reread the short article over and over. According to Malcolm, Wilcom was TGO? She took a deep breath. She knew that a lot of companies changed their name and "relaunched" when something had happened that could put a dent in their public reputation. Hell, she'd known one contractor to change its name to an unpronounceable series of letters, presumably to stop people talking about them.

Well, at least she knew what the penalty would be for talking to anyone about her suspicions.

The phone rang, startling her again. She looked at the screen. It was Colonel Duke Cameron. Her heart sped up, and she didn't know if it was because of the stupid crush she'd had on him when she was in a neighboring squadron or if it was about all the PreCall problems she suspected but couldn't reveal.

"Hi. This is Duke. Can you spare me a few minutes and come up to my office?"

Oh God. She looked at her phone screen again as if it may have the answer to all her problems. She hesitated. She couldn't tell him anything. She had to be really careful.

"Sure! I can be there in five?"

"Perfect. See you in a minute," his said in his smooth, low-toned voice.

She stood on the tarmac, wondering if anything could happen that would prevent her from having to face Colonel Cameron. A lightning strike? A heart attack? Nothing.

If only she didn't have suspicions that her company had caused the crash. If this were any other day, any other place, finally out of uniform, she could have set about getting him out on a date. She had crushed on him from afar for over three years while she was a pilot in the air force. It wasn't one of those crazy fixations that she taken with her everywhere she went, but every time she had seen him while they were both officers, she had always entertained the "what-if."

But today wasn't the day to pursue that. She took a deep breath and a long blink against the sunlight, steeling herself for the meeting. She was going to have to lie to him, and she wasn't looking forward to that.

She strode into the office building again, put her jacket back on, and turned her phone off. Malcolm had given her the idea that TGO could be listening to her, or tracking her, or something. Cameron's executive assistant, Captain Moss, opened his office door for her.

"It's been a long time," Duke said with a smile, gesturing to the seat in front of his desk.

"I can't believe how excited I was when I heard I'd be coming back to Red Flag, but now . . . I just don't know."

"I feel the same," he said. "But right now, I really need an update on how your search and rescue is going. Do you have any new information?"

"They've sent a lot of people out there, eight sorties in total I believe. No sign yet."

"That's what I can't believe. We had the location of at least one aircraft, but nobody's found the pilots?"

"It seems not. They would have told us, obviously, if they had."

"And you don't think that's strange? Why is TGO so determined to do search and rescue today when we have a unit of pararescuers on-site?" Cameron leaned forward and put his elbows on his desk, spreading out his hands in appeal. "Wouldn't you want the pararescuers to come for you?"

She hesitated, trying to figure out a response that wouldn't get her into trouble, either with her company or with Duke. She watched as he picked up a pen and started tapping it furiously on his desk. That wasn't a good sign either.

"TGO has the best SAR in the industry, and we have the best technology." She tried to speak confidently, because she was speaking the truth. But still, she had a thought stuck in the back of her mind that if it had been their technology that had caused the planes to crash, they might also be looking to destroy the evidence.

He stared at her for a long time before saying anything, and she struggled not to fill the silence with any kind of blabber that might give her away.

"Let's get together later at the officers' club. We can catch up, maybe grab some nachos," he said, thankfully before she let anything slip.

Her heart leapt in her chest. Did she have a date? Or was he going to grill her about TGO? If only he'd asked yesterday, under totally different circumstances. "I'd like that. What time?"

"Seven?" he suggested.

"It's a date." She'd be optimistic.

They shook hands, and she left, passing another colonel who was asking Duke's exec to make time to see him on an urgent matter. She swiveled her head as she passed, wondering what his urgent matter was. Could it be something to do with the crash?

Maybe he'd tell her tonight. Maybe she could trust him with what she knew or what she thought she knew. But was it worth her career, and maybe every cent she earned from that day onward?

Was TGO really that vindictive? Or was Malcolm just being dramatic?

CHAPTER THIRTEEN

Conrad tugged at the sleeves of his blues jacket before being shown into Colonel Duke Cameron's office. He recognized the woman who was leaving as he arrived; he just couldn't place her. Damn, he was getting old.

"Good to see you," Cameron said.

"You too. Who was that who just left? I think I recognize her." Conrad took the offered chair in front of Cameron's desk.

"That was Casey Jacobs. You probably ran into her at a previous Red Flag when she was an MC-130J pilot. She left a couple of years ago and got a job with TGO," Cameron said, straightening the pens on his desk.

"Oh, I see. Yes, maybe that's where I know her from. So, she's TGO now?"

Cameron regarded him steadily from across the desk. "Yes, she is. Why?"

It was now or never. "My weapons officer, Major Malden, has been taken into custody by TGO. Do you know anything about that?" Conrad leaned forward, putting his elbows on his knees and trying not to grip his hands too tightly together.

Cameron sighed. "I heard. That had nothing to do with me. General Daniels gave the order, and TGO carried it out. Although, I will say that what he's asked for—house arrest—isn't exactly legal under the uniform code of military justice."

"What does that mean?" Conrad asked.

"It means that she's confined to barracks, but there's no actual law that says she has to stay there." Colonel Cameron swiveled in his chair and gazed out his window. "I don't know for sure, but I suspect that General Daniels was trying to give her a little leeway without alerting TGO."

Conrad took a breath and prepared himself for the moment he put his career, and Missy's, on the line. "Can we speak off the record?" he asked.

"As long as you are not confessing to a crime," Cameron replied with a slight smile.

Conrad hesitated. In some respects he *was* confessing to a crime.

At his hesitation, Cameron frowned and closed his eyes. "Tell me you had nothing to do with this."

"Oh God no! Of course I didn't. But neither did Major Malden." Conrad looked to his hands, and then sat back in his seat and held Cameron's gaze steadily.

"And how exactly do you know that?"

"Well, firstly, I know her. I've flown with her for years.

I know she would never do anything that has been suggested she might do. And secondly"—he closed his eyes briefly—"she was with me most of the night."

Cameron frowned. "Well, why didn't you say so to begin with?"

Conrad stared at him meaningfully and raised his eyebrows.

Awareness washed over Cameron's expression. "Oh. You mean she was *with* you."

"Yes," he said. His heart started racing, wondering what the colonel's reaction would be.

"You're having a relationship with your weapons officer? How long has it been going on?" Cameron leaned forward and again, arranged and rearranged the pens on his desk, to the nearest millimeter.

"I'm not...I wasn't...We're not having a relationship." For fuck's sake. Why was he suddenly stammering like a teenager? "It was the first time we'd..." He let his voice trail off.

"Sweet Jesus. You were with her all night?"

"Let me start at the beginning." Conrad took a breath and told him everything he knew about TGO—especially the man who had followed Missy into the hotel—plus the golf cart in the hangar, and about the lipstick graffiti on Eleanor's aircraft. He couldn't believe he had only just remembered that. And then he confessed that Missy had left his bed before he awoke.

Cameron nodded, and that morphed into him shaking

his head at Conrad. "So really you've got nothing, except somebody writing 'bitch' on Eleanor's aircraft, TGO employees in a hangar—for which, until we find Eleanor Daniels, you only have Major Malden's word for—and a TGO employee going into lodging at the same time as her. It's hardly concrete."

This was exactly why Missy hadn't spoken up herself. Conrad dropped his head for a second and then nodded.

"I have Major Malden's file here," Cameron said. "What can you tell me about her parents or her family?"

Conrad was taken aback. "I don't...Nothing, really." He kicked himself again. Why didn't he know anything about her background?

"What about anything that happened to her before she enlisted?" Cameron asked.

"You mean commissioned, not enlisted. She is an officer." Conrad's patience was nearing its end.

"No, I mean enlisted. She was given a choice at the age of seventeen: enlist in the military or go to juvie."

He sat back in his chair, aghast. How did he not know this about her? He didn't even know who she really was. He'd never asked her about her family, or school, or her degree. Nothing. He really didn't know her at all.

"She had a hard life before the air force," Cameron said, tapping one of his meticulously placed pens on Missy's file. "She worked hard, got a degree, and was commissioned as a second lieutenant. You've only known her for the past four years of her life. You have no idea what she is capable of, and neither do I. So don't go putting your career, or your liberty, on the line for someone you don't seem to know that well." He stood and opened his office door. "I think we can both carefully consider what we've heard today, can't we, Colonel?"

Conrad stood quickly, tugged at his sleeves again, and left, pausing only to say, "Yes, sir." He strode out of Cameron's office, kicking himself. It was exactly as Missy had anticipated.

Missy. How had he known so little about her? Why hadn't she talked about her past? Why had she kept him in the dark for all these years? The truth was, he didn't know anything about her at all, and despite it being his fault, it was beginning to freak him out.

As he walked past other airmen, saluting and offering a morning greeting to each, he couldn't help but notice that everyone was taking this accident personally. No one smiled; no one looked happy, or lighthearted, or even distracted.

He wished he could join the Animal's posse. Nothing would clear his mind and make him feel better than leaving the base and going to look for Eleanor and Dex. If push came to shove, he would smuggle Missy out of Nellis and...He didn't know what would happen after that. Going on the run sounded a little unstructured to him.

Sergeant Cripps was loitering outside the lodging when Conrad walked up. "Sir, they're taking Major Malden to the MP's office to be questioned. I thought you'd want to know."

"Thank you, Sergeant. Is there anyone there..." How could he put this to an enlisted man?

"...who can help you? Who's not in TGO's pocket? Sure. Sergeant April Heron. She'll tell you what's going on." Cripps wrote her name on his notebook and tore out the page to give him.

"April Heron. Got it. Thanks." General Patton was right: enlisted men are cunning and should be watched. For the first time in what felt like ages, he smiled.

Missy and Colonel Janke were staring at each other in her holding cell. She knew she'd made the right call. He was supposed to be her JAG—her advocate—and yet he was threatening her? Why was he looking so panicked? "I want a new JAG," she repeated.

His fists clenched by his side, and she wondered if she'd gone so far down the insubordination road that she wouldn't be able to make her way back. But she held her ground, and his gaze.

"Why don't you just tell me the extent of the conversation Major Daniels shared with you? The one she had with her father. What did she say happened?" The slight manic look in his eyes didn't invite the sharing of confidences. Who was this man?

This was about Eleanor and her father? About the conversation she'd had about the men in the hangar?

Several things clicked into place inside her brain. But she knew enough not to give anything away.

He picked up her file from the table and left without a word, slamming the door, making her jump.

What the hell was going on here?

Whatever it was had to do with the men she'd seen in their hangar the first evening of Red Flag—when she and Eleanor had been shooting the shit about men and other pilots. It had been only two days ago, but already it felt like another lifetime.

A female sergeant came to escort her back to her room in the stale-smelling barracks. When she opened the door for her, Missy's mouth dropped open. Instead of the cot bed, there was a proper bed—made with sheets and a blanket and a proper pillow. There was a jug of water and a glass on top of a chest of drawers.

"I got someone to bring some essentials for you. I don't care what TGO says; there is a minimum level of care we offer to people confined to barracks," the sergeant said.

"Thank you so much. What's your name, Sergeant?"

"April Heron, ma'am. Just shout if you need anything." The woman turned away and closed the door behind her.

Missy looked into the chest of drawers. Someone had brought her PT clothes, an extra uniform, and her underwear. A towel and her washbag were in the second drawer, and in the third was another washbag. She frowned. Had they accidentally packed Eleanor's bag too?

She pulled it out and opened it. Inside was her Kindle,

her phone, and her charger that fit both, two Twinkies, some pretzels, some jerky, and...She closed her eyes. Someone had packed a brand-new vibrator for her. Conrad, of course. At least she hoped so. Not that she wanted to see him, but the thought of someone else putting it there was just plain creepy. Where the hell had he gotten that on lockdown?

She unwrapped a Twinkie and picked up her phone—it was dead. She plugged it in and ate the disgusting, delicious, sweet treat in two mouthfuls. Within seconds her phone started bleeping with notifications. Most were notifications from Facebook friends. One wasn't.

>> *I'm coming to get you at lights-out.*

It was from Conrad, and literally the first message on her phone from him that didn't just consist of the time for their flight briefing. It was the only time he'd actually used his words.

How had he gone from zero to a hundred in the space of a day? How had she? She was still pissed at him, though. He was still the self-absorbed guy who had put him and his own career ahead of hers. And that's assuming he thought about her career at all.

A tiny part of her considered fleeing for the first time since she was seventeen. When the judge had given the choice between military boot camp and detention, she'd considered running. She'd had nothing and no one to stay for, and just about everything she owned could have fit in her backpack. Even now she was surprised, and thankful, that she'd made a different choice. She was going to make that same choice again. She was going to choose herself, her career, the air force, and everything she'd worked toward. She wasn't going to cave and run from something she didn't do. For a mistake.

It wasn't a mistake. You did this to yourself by breaking the rules. None of this would be happening if you'd kept your head down and your hands off Conrad.

She lay on her new bed and pushed out a deep sigh. It was so much more comfortable than the cot from last night. She had a lot of questions for Conrad. A lot of stuff that she would have to get him to do. She had a plan.

Kind of. She picked up her Kindle and tried to read, but her brain refused to leave the possibility that she would be sent to jail for the rest of her life.

CHAPTER FOURTEEN

Conrad had been sweet-talking Sergeant April Heron the whole day, not that she needed much encouragement to support Missy over TGO. Pretty much everyone he talked to suspected they were sketchy. But no one had proof, and he had to be careful that word didn't get back to them that he was going around base trash-talking them. It didn't seem as if they took kindly to obstacles.

It was no secret that plenty of military contractors cut corners to bolster profits. But for all the accolades they had gotten for sponsoring Red Flag, nearly everyone was beginning to wish the exercise had been completely canceled. As was he.

This Red Flag had been an unmitigated disaster. Missy had decided to leave him, and he'd realized just how badly he'd been treating her—even though he was doing it for the best reasons. But now that they'd had sex, that reason had ceased to exist. All this time that he hadn't asked about her life, hadn't socialized with her, had kept her at bay with ridiculous lies about the women he was supposedly fucking every night, all those things were to keep her at arm's length. Something inside him had always known that getting closer to her would be fatal to both their careers. Okay, to *his* career. Yup, he'd been an ass. And if it wasn't for this shitting Red Flag, he could have continued in his ignorance. Except she'd obviously made the decision before they'd even come here. Shit. He clenched his fists.

He waited on the picnic table in the playground—the one that he'd remember forever—for the lights to go out at the barracks. As soon as they did, he hefted his backpack onto his back and waited for the half-assed sentry to go inside for coffee or whatever he did before his rounds.

He knocked at Missy's window, and she opened it for him without a word. He shoved his backpack in and then jumped up onto the window ledge and fed his way through the small opening.

"Evening," he said when he had both feet on the ground.

"Good evening, sir," she said sassily.

He shook his head. "Okay. I have supplies." He unzipped his backpack and brought out a four-pack of ice-cold Stella Artois and a lime.

"How did you know I drank that? You've never once seen me drink that," she said, disbelief in her voice.

"That's not all, baby." He reached in and pulled out a thermal bag and handed it to her.

She sniffed it and moaned, which in turn sent a frisson of memory through him.

"Where in the world did you find a döner kebab here?" she whispered as she tore open the wrapping.

"Easy, tiger, one of those is for me." He caught the white paper bag she threw at him.

She took a bite and her eyes closed in what he could only describe as ecstasy. It was only just hitting him how alike sex and eating were. At least, they certainly seemed to invoke the same feelings in Missy.

She took a few bites, grease and onion falling from her mouth. He shoved some napkins at her and she put the kebab down next to her on the bed and mopped up. "Seriously. How did you know you just hit my sweet spot?"

He reined himself in from saying the double entendre that was on his lips. "I knew I'd find someone here who had been stationed with you somewhere. The problem was, I didn't know where you'd been stationed before." He held his hands up. "I know, my bad. Anyway, I found a guy who used to fly from Incirlik to Ramstein when you were there. He said you were the döner queen of the squadron. He also remembered your drink of choice."

"It's true, I took my crown seriously. I can not only find the best döner in any city, but I can also make them. I just haven't had one in ages."

From a different section of his pack, he withdrew two notepads and a bunch of pens he'd stolen from the briefing room. "As requested."

She'd already stuffed another mouthful of kebab in her mouth, so she just nodded at him and gave him a thumbs-up.

He popped the tops on the Stella and with his pocketknife cut the lime into pieces and stuck a piece in hers.

No way was he going to wreck good beer with citrus. She was a freak.

He sat on the floor, next to the chest of drawers, facing her, and dug into his own kebab, enjoying the silence between them. He wasn't even sure they'd ever eaten together before, aside from shoving sandwiches in their faces in the briefing rooms between missions.

Neither of them said anything. Occasionally their eyes met as they ate, and a warmth between them bloomed as her eyes smiled at him.

It was a picture he'd keep locked away for a long time. Missy, the object of all his attention and deliberate nonattention, with grease on her face and bits of onion and lettuce hanging out of her mouth, but with her eyes shining in the light from the streetlamps outside.

He wiped his mouth when he finished. She was still attacking the last half of her meal, so he decided to take the initiative. "Okay, so I realized that I've been a bad friend these past few years. I don't know much about you, not where you're from, nothing about your family—if you even have one—nothing about your past before we started to work together. And I want to know you. Properly. I want to be able to anticipate your every move, the way you do mine. I want to see you. Try to understand you. Okay?"

She suddenly looked self-conscious. She held her hand over her mouth and grabbed for the napkins. Was she choking? Or was she going to cry?

She finally swallowed her mouthful and wrapped the

tissues and the last remnants of her döner that had fallen on her lap and put them back in the white paper bag. She balled it up and lobbed it into the trash can in the corner of the room.

"Swish," she said as it went straight in, no rebound or anything.

"See? I didn't know you could do that."

She twisted her mouth into a smile and scooched back on the bed, so she was leaning against the wall. She took a mouthful of beer and shook her head. "I'm honestly not sure if you deserve to know anything about me."

"You're right. I definitely don't." He nodded and waited for her to reply.

She said nothing, just took another swig of her stupid citrus beer.

"Okay, how about I tell you a secret about me first." He was really going to tell her. It was now or never.

Her eyebrows rose, but still she said nothing. She was a hard audience. And he deserved no less.

"Do you remember the nurse in Colorado? The swimming instructor in Norfolk? The waitress, also in Norfolk? The lawyer in Virginia Beach? The—"

"The archaeologist from Penn State, the stripper from . . . okay, I can't remember where she was from, the gymnast from two days ago? Of course I do."

He took a breath. "Yeah. None of them were real."

She blinked a bunch of times and her mouth dropped open. "What?"

"None of them."

She frowned and stared, for the first time seemingly at a loss for words. Or scheming his imminent death. It was hard to tell with Missy. "But why?"

And that was the sticky part. Because he was only just figuring it out for himself. "Because I didn't want to fall in love with you. I didn't want you to fall in love with me—" he began.

"What, so if you weren't sleeping around, I would one hundred percent just roll over and fall in love with you? Let me tell you this, Conrad: You're not that charming. You're barely charming at all, actually." She looked annoyed. And when she put it like that, she was right to be.

"Look, I know 'sorry' barely covers it, but my motives were pure. At least, they probably weren't exactly pure, but . . . well maybe *good* is a better word. I didn't want to socialize with the squadron, when I knew I'd be in close proximity to you. I know it's stupid—trust me, I've been over this in my head a thousand times—and it makes not a whole lot of sense to me either, but in my defense, I don't think I exactly knew why I was doing it either at the time."

"Well that just makes you stupid." She was staring at her beer bottle and pulling strips of damp label from it and chucking them onto the floor.

"Do you forgive me?" he asked, at a loss for anything else to say.

"I don't know. It's too early to say and too soon to process," she said, finally meeting his eyes.

He thought—no, really he had just hoped—that she would jump into his arms in delight. But deep down he kind of knew she was too smart for that. He needed to pay for misleading her.

"So why do you want to know about me now? What's changed?" she asked.

"Everything's changed. Everything. You're leaving me. No, you chose to leave me, and that just about kills me. That we knew each other so poorly. That I lied to you. That I did everything to push you away, even though you literally never showed any interest in me." He paused, suddenly realizing what a complete and total ass he'd been. Like, on fucking multiple levels.

A silence fell between them again. "So what do you want to know?" she asked, lobbing a pillow at him.

He deflected it before it hit him in the face. She did throw with extraordinary accuracy. "Tell me how you came into the military." It was a test, and he hated himself for it. But he needed to know if she was open to being truthful with him, now that he'd bared his soul.

She laughed and looked up at the ceiling. She nodded a few times to herself, and his heart clenched, hoping she wasn't thinking up a lie.

"Honestly? A very nice judge told me to enlist in the military or go to jail. So, being the rebellious pisser I was, I chose the greater of the two evils."

Conrad laughed, a release, and a sliver of happiness shot through the emotional mess that was stuffing up his brain.

"Jail? What happened?" he asked.

"My parents kept bugging out on me through my high school years, so I kind of bugged out on school too. I managed to graduate, eventually. It was that spring break before I was supposed to graduate that I got caught trespassing with some friends...and, well, the owner of the factory had donated heavily to the county sheriff, so we got charged. Three months in a correctional facility, or graduate school and enlist. So off to boot camp I went. Two years later I'd completed a degree in applied math and was commissioned as an officer. And then four years later I met you."

"You got arrested after one offense?" he asked. "Where *was* this?"

She grinned. "Oh, no. That was maybe my sixteenth offense. And it was in Sacramento."

"I can't believe it. When we first met, you had this reputation of being a squared away, by-the-book officer. I would never have imagined you had such a delinquent past." He tipped his head to one side, as if considering. "Actually, yes, I can." He winked at her and she gave him the finger, making him laugh out loud.

"What do you do when you're not at work?" he asked.

"I ride my horses. I go out with friends. I see movies..." She spread her hands. "Like everyone else."

"You have horses?" he said, slapping his hand against his forehead. "How did I not know...Jesus, I'm sorry. What a jackass I am. I really didn't ask you anything about you, did I?" Could the depths of his misery get any worse?

"Well don't get me started on my conspiracy theory website, my thirteen cats, or my visceral need to live-tweet every episode of *Real Housewives*...," she said earnestly. "I wrote a post about the truth behind the Bermuda Triangle and that one guy from *Jersey Shore* totally reposted it on his site."

What? He hesitated just a second before realizing that she was putting him on in a big way. "Dude. You nearly had me there."

"I really did, didn't I?" she said with a smile.

Silence fell between them. There was so much more that he wanted to know, but he didn't know how to ask. "Shall we return to the elephant in the room?"

"You mean the fact that I'm actually in this room?" she asked with a sigh. "Yeah. There's stuff I need to talk to you about. There's a guy—Colonel Janke—who came to me claiming to be my JAG. He was a douche-canoe and when I asked for a different lawyer, he kind of freaked out. He insisted on knowing what Eleanor had told me about the conversation with her father. I didn't tell him anything, but—"

"Wait. In our meeting with the general, when you mentioned the guy in the hangar and the conversation Eleanor had with her father about it, that was when our whole conversation went to shit. The way Danvers put his hand on the general's shoulder almost seemed threatening instead of supportive."

"Right?" Missy said. "That's what I thought too. So, you think this whole shit show is about the conversation Eleanor had with her father? It must have been about the guy in the hangar—the one who approached me outside lodging." She averted her eyes as if she was trying to piece everything together.

He'd never admit it, but he definitely owed that guy. He was the one who literally put Missy into his arms. "Maybe he's the key to all of this."

Missy opened her mouth to say something, but his phone rang. He answered quick as he could to suppress the noise.

"Animal?"

Missy looked anxiously at the door, expecting someone to come in, but no one did. She opened one of the notepads and wrote some notes to herself as Conrad talked to the Animal. God only knew what the crazy pilot wanted at this time of night.

Conrad ended the call and took a deep breath. "The Animal took out a team and found Eleanor."

"Oh thank God. Is she okay?" She blew out air in relief.

"She's alive, but not okay. They medivaced her to the city hospital. The RAF pilot is dehydrated and injured, but he's being brought back to the base hospital. It took them an hour to find them." His eyes squinted.

"What? A bunch of pilots found them in an hour, but TGO's search and rescue couldn't do it in over twenty-four?"

"Or didn't want to," he said.

"I can't believe that. If we're saying seriously that they caused the crash and then tried to leave them out there in the desert, then they won't think twice about getting rid of me too." Her voice was grim, and stressed-sounding even to her ears.

"I'm not going to let anything happen to you. You're my wingman. Anyone will have to go through me to get to you." He said the words simply, as if they were just plain old fact.

She got up and looked at him. "Thank you," she said. "But in case this is our last moment together . . ." She let her words drift off for dramatic effect.

His arms wrapped around her, and she dropped her head back to kiss him. Nothing would feel safer than being in his arms. But he gently disengaged. "Nice try, but slightly overdramatic. I've got to go, but Sergeant Heron will be looking out for you while I'm gone, and when she has to leave the facility, she has recruited someone else to watch TGO around here.

"I've also got a special investigator to come speak to you first thing. He seems to be a good guy. One of ours. Call if you need anything, but, you know, hide your phone. Yours and Eleanor's room had been ransacked when I got there this afternoon. They may go through all your stuff here too."

Her blood rose at the thought of a TGO guy riffling through her clothes and belongings. Not to mention

Eleanor's. "I really want to see Eleanor," she said, stepping back from them.

"I'll put out some feelers and see when and if she can have visitors. But prepare yourself for the worst. She wasn't in good shape when they found her."

She nodded. "You really can't stay?" She hated how small her voice sounded.

"I want to stay. But this evening was about döners and beer and trying to get to know you a bit better. I know things are complicated right now, but I can do better work out there."

She nodded again.

"I've got to go. Oh, I brought these, in case you really can't live without me." He pulled two AA batteries out of his pocket.

She looked at them, perplexed, until she realized that they were for the vibrator. "Get out!" she hissed. "And take your batteries with you!"

He grinned and hugged her one more time, kissing her on the forehead. She punched his arm in response. She had no idea what was going on with them now. He seemed to be ignoring the conversation they'd had. But it was true she needed all the friends she could get.

She went to sleep saying prayers for Eleanor. Hoping the morning would bring good news.

CHAPTER FIFTEEN

The morning brought more than good news about Eleanor. It also brought good news in the form of the special investigator that Conrad had mentioned the night before.

The U.S. Air Force Office of Special Investigations handled everything except petty crime. They were the NCIS of the air force. Major Harris Bowman visited her in her room and briefed her on his investigation.

Nothing good was going on there at Nellis, and the thought that anyone figured she'd had something to do with it burned her.

But Bowman was a good guy. She could tell that from the start. He told her they'd been looking at a certain contractor who had been caught on the base's closed-circuit cameras several times at all hours of the day and night.

"If there are cameras, can't they see who entered the hangars?" she asked, confused.

Major Bowman sighed. "The cameras only cover the two banks on base, the gas station, and the McDonald's."

"So, the important things, then," she said in exasperation. "Touch an aircraft if you like, but God help you if you touch a hamburger?"

"Something like that," he admitted.

He asked her to corroborate what Conrad had already told him, and she confessed that it was nothing except conjecture. She couldn't prove anything.

He left and said he'd be back shortly.

Missy felt good after their talk. It was comforting that someone here other than Conrad believed someone else may have been responsible for tampering with Eleanor's aircraft.

Nevertheless, when he returned an hour later, he was escorted by Lieutenant Colonel Janke. Fear spiked in her belly as he entered her room at the barracks. Just having him in proximity to her personal belongings made her twitch.

"Colonel Janke is here as an observer," Major Bowman said. "It's a courtesy my office has extended to him."

"We've met," Missy said shortly.

Janke said nothing, but it worried her how at ease he seemed. Nothing like the panic he'd shown the day before.

"Can you tell me what you saw in the hangar?" Bowman asked.

"When I was with Eleanor?" she asked.

Bowman nodded, but Janke suddenly looked startled and kept looking between them as if in shock.

"We went to our hangar that evening and found it

locked. At first we thought the general had provided the lock so that the crews didn't have to watch the aircraft at night, but an airman took the lock away when he opened it for us. As the hangar door was opening, three men came out on a golf cart. As I told General Daniels, I could identify at least one of them again."

Bowman was making notes and didn't say anything immediately.

Janke butted in. "What did he look like? Did he have glasses? Black hair? Was he short?"

Missy glared at him. He was none of those things, and she wondered if he was deliberately trying to mess with her memory of the man. "I could pick him out of a lineup. I mean, if he has base access, there will be a photo in our system for his pass."

Janke looked worried. "What? You can just point at a random photo to get yourself off the hook? Right. That's not going to fly. Right, Major?" He looked at Bowman for support.

"Actually, that works for me," Bowman said. "Pack your things and go back to your room, Major. I got permission from Colonel Cameron last night to release you from house arrest, although you—along with everyone else—will be confined to base. Please come to my office at fifteen hundred hours to go through our pass photos."

"Thank you, Major Bowman. I'd be happy to. The guy in the hangar definitely wasn't military, by the way. His hair was too long."

He pursed his lips and nodded thoughtfully. "A contractor, then?"

"I think so. Maybe TGO." She fought the desire to look at Janke to see how he was faring under Colonel Cameron's order, until she couldn't resist the urge any longer. She glanced over at him to find him clamping his lips together, but not angrily. It was almost as if he were trying not to smile. The man had some weapon-grade crazy going on.

She really didn't care anymore; Janke was Bowman's problem now. She just wanted to get the hell out of Dodge, pack her shit, and head off to her new assignment.

Conrad, of course, was a different matter.

CHAPTER SIXTEEN

Chris Grove was setting his endgame into play. When you knew how the military worked, it was all too easy.

His number one problem was not being able to get rid of Major Malden while she'd been in protective custody. That had been Mr. Danvers's mistake. He shouldn't have pressured General Daniels to find a scapegoat. If she'd been left alone, she would have been fair game for him.

And he'd spent a pleasant hour or so figuring out how to do it. Up close and personal had been his choice. Very close, and very personal. A tingle of excitement shot through him as he remembered his various kill plans. Having it look like a sex crime, a random shooting in Vegas, an ugly accident. He'd gone over all the possibilities many times.

But Danvers had given him other orders. As much as he appreciated what Mr. Danvers had done for him, he knew this was a mistake. He knew he was the only one who could kill her without any blowback. But no. Danvers had given the job to someone else to "cement their loyalty," whatever that meant.

But as soon as she was out of house arrest and free to go wherever she wanted on base, she'd be easy to kill. But maybe not for a rookie. Grove had already decided to cover the shooter, just in case he fucked it up. Everyone thinks they can kill someone. Few actually have the balls for it. Especially in cold blood. So he was going to play backup to make sure nothing went wrong.

Because something always went wrong.

Missy managed to keep busy and on the move all that morning and most of the afternoon. She didn't want to give Conrad any chance to catch up to her, mainly because she didn't want to discuss their future. If being suspected of sabotage had taught her one thing, it was not to plan too far ahead.

Back at her lodging, having packed the last of her ransacked belongings into her backpack, she separated Eleanor's into two bags. One had all her uniforms, and the smaller satchel had underwear, comfortable T-shirts and pants, her phone, computer, and washbag.

As she packed the last of Eleanor's belongings into her bags, she paused. She felt as if she were packing up a deceased airman's belongings, like she'd had to do once for a fallen sister in Qatar. She felt cold inside, as if her going through the motions of packing away Eleanor's stuff would somehow make it okay if she died.

She shivered, unable to separate the anxiety she felt for Eleanor's prognosis, and her own legal prognosis.

She left the backpacks with the captain in the next door room—she really didn't want to have to think about anyone going through her stuff again—and took the satchel with her to Major Bowman's office.

She was looking forward to identifying the guy and letting Bowman pick him up. Not that they had anything concrete on him. She hesitated outside his building. They really didn't have anything on him at all. A chance meeting at the base lodging after she'd seen him in their hangar—for which she was sure he'd have an excuse—and that was it.

What if Bowman let the TGO guy go? What if he went looking for Missy again? Her stomach churned.

Bowman was waiting for her. She handed over Eleanor's satchel and asked if he could arrange to have it sent to the hospital. He left it with the MPs who were rotating to the hospital to guard her door.

Bowman had an interview room ready, which sent trickles of anxiety through her again. She wondered if this was some kind of bait and switch, to avoid having to really arrest her. Release her from house arrest, ask her to "help them with their inquiries," and then show "proof" that she'd done something wrong and arrest her.

She hesitated at the doorway, her stomach turning in knots. Suddenly she felt that if she took a step into the room, that would be it.

"It's okay. I'll leave the door open," Bowman said, rolling his eyes. "I'm not going to arrest you."

"Isn't that what someone would say if they were trying to trick someone?" she countered.

"I suppose so, but look." He raised his hands, both of which held paper cups of coffee. A small tablet was under one elbow. "I wouldn't usher you into one of our beating rooms armed with just a coffee, now, would I?"

"You have beating rooms? What the . . . ?" She stepped back from the door, suddenly disorientated.

He rolled his eyes at her again and brushed past her. He put the coffees on the table and sat at one of the chairs. "Come on. Sit down for God's sake. This coffee is bearable hot, but downright nasty when it's cold. You can trust me on that." He then ignored her for a few seconds while he opened up an application on the tablet.

Missy cursed herself for being so ridiculously skittish and joined him at the table. He turned the tablet toward her. "Here are all the passes issued to contractors in the past month. We have about fifteen different companies working here for Red Flag: TGO, of course, but also catering folk, janitorial services, waste disposal, et cetera et cetera," he said. "There were five hundred and seventy-three temporary base passes issued that were still live in the system at the start of the exercise.

She nodded. "I actually had no idea it was so complicated running Red Flag," she said, looking at the first page of six photos.

"The base basically triples its occupancy, so we have to

bring in help." He sat back in his chair and watched her go through the photos.

She swiped left to keep them coming, in what, in some alternate reality, would have been the worst dating site ever, until she saw the picture of the man with long hair and implant teeth. "Him. He's the one Eleanor and I saw coming out of our hangar, and he's the one who tried to talk to me outside lodging when I was about to come to the hangar for the night." She expanded the picture of his pass with her fingers. "Chris Grove. TGO."

Bowman slid the tablet away from Missy, spun it around, and looked at the photo. "Yup. That was the guy we were tracking on the base cameras."

"I'd hardly call that conclusive evidence," a voice came from the door.

Janke. She swore she heard Bowman groan under his breath.

Both Bowman and Missy stood up out of respect for the man who outranked them both.

"No, sir. It's not conclusive at all," Bowman said evenly.

Janke ignored him. "Congratulations on your release, Major Malden. I couldn't be happier for you. It must be such a relief to be able to put all this behind you."

Startled, Missy turned to look at him. "Yes, sir," was all she could bring herself to say. What a weird man he was. Maybe his job was being devil's advocate? But that didn't explain his interrogation of her when she'd first been brought from General Daniels's office.

"What are your plans now? Are you staying here or heading home?" he asked casually, as if they were chitchatting at a wedding.

Wow, dude did *not* know how to speak to people naturally. "I don't know, sir," she said, fairly truthfully.

He nodded and walked away from the doorway.

"I wish I'd closed the door now," Bowman said.

"Who *is* he?" she asked.

"I don't know. Some legal guy. The general sent him to my office to 'observe' how we handled the investigation into the crashes. I told him I wouldn't be investigating them, because that sort of investigation belongs to the NTSB. But he insisted I start investigating in order to find the culprit, even before they'd found the aircraft." He shrugged. "At least now I can get on with my normal job."

"So do you think this guy is involved?" she asked hopefully, looking at the screen

"Involved in something. I certainly have enough to bring him in for questioning. The RAF pilot—Flight Lieutenant Dexter Stone—is being debriefed by the British authorities at the moment, so we don't have access to him. But as soon as we do, and if he can ID Chris Grove, too, we should have enough to hold him."

"That's a relief. So am I free to go home? I'm guessing the rest of Red Flag will be canceled?" she asked.

"I guess. As soon as the lockdown's been lifted." He shrugged and stood up. "Thank you for your help, and I apologize for any inconvenience." He held out his hand and she shook it.

She left the MP's office feeling like a load had been taken off her shoulders. She felt fidgety, though, maybe because she hadn't worked out for a few days.

Finally she felt free to remedy that.

Free.

When Conrad heard that Cameron had given the okay to release Missy, he went to find out what had happened to change his mind. Hopefully that meant they'd figured out what had happened to cause the crash and had exonerated Missy. Then he'd go find her and brief her on what he'd found out. Maybe he could be the hero today and be the one to tell her that she was totally home free from suspicion and jail time.

Rumors had been spreading so wildly since the British pilot had returned with Eleanor that the cause of their crash could have been anything from a suicide pact to the Russians infiltrating Red Flag. Conrad believed none of it but was beginning to realize how powerful some information was, when there was no official information released. The grapevine was choking off all rational thought to the base.

One airman in the air traffic control room had even been accused of being one of the Russian spies and had been taken into custody. First as a precaution, and then when his innocence was established, for his own protection. The base was going crazy. Cameron needed to talk to the airman confined to base to avoid anything awful happening.

He really needed to stop those rumors and put out some official word.

The fact that all this was happening on base, and Cameron had not made an announcement or given a briefing, gave Conrad pause. There must be more to this than met the eye. Even though what met the eye was already pretty fucking crazy.

He made his way over to the main administration block that overlooked the runway—the nicest offices for the highest brass.

He had been there only the day previously, but already everything seemed different. In some offices, people were standing around talking; in others, phones were ringing off the hook. If Conrad didn't know any better, he would have assumed the apocalypse was coming. Perhaps he didn't know any better.

He reached Cameron's office and knocked on the doorjamb of the open door. The boss's executive, Captain Olivia Moss, looked up and heaved a sigh of relief. "Colonel Conrad, I'm so happy to see you."

"You are? That's always good to hear, but why?"

"I'm just . . . I don't know . . ." She took a deep breath "I feel as if I'm hanging on to order with a very, very thin thread. Everyone wants to know something. And I can't find anyone who knows anything."

"I'm looking for Colonel Cameron. Have you seen him?" Conrad leaned against the wall opposite her desk.

"I haven't. No one has since yesterday. And he's not picking up his home phone, his DSL line, and his cell phone goes straight to voice mail." The DSL line was a secure telephone and data line that some high-ranking airmen had in their homes. It made it doubly strange that he was not picking up a call.

"Maybe he's in one of the sit-rep rooms? Maybe he's being briefed? Or maybe he's getting a brief from the Pentagon. That would explain his absence and his lack of communication." Conrad didn't know why he was trying to make her feel better; really, he wanted her to panic as much as everyone else. Maybe panic was what was needed among the officers in the building to get something done about the situation on base. "I need to speak to him too."

Captain Moss held up her notebook. "As of now, you are number"—she ran her finger to the bottom of the list— "twenty-eight. And that's just in the last two hours."

"What about General Daniels? He's the only person on base who ranks higher than Colonel Cameron, right?" Conrad asked.

"Right, but he was pulled back to the Pentagon last night, after they found his daughter."

What? That was strange. "I can't believe he left before Eleanor and the British pilot were debriefed. Didn't he want to know what had happened?" Half of him expected her to look shocked, but instead she bit her lip and nodded to the open door.

He raised his eyebrows and closed the door, wondering what she would say.

"I don't know. I was here when they told him they'd been found. I expected him to demand to know what had happened. But he didn't. He literally packed his briefcase and told his exec to book them on the next flight to DC. I don't think he even went to the hospital to see his daughter."

Jesus. He was either a terrible father, and a terrible general, or there was an unspeakable alternative where he already knew what had happened to his daughter in the desert.

When Conrad figured out Captain Moss didn't know anything else, he officially made himself number twenty-eight on Cameron's list and left. As he was walking down the corridor, a thought occurred to him, and he turned around and returned to Cameron's office.

He put his head through the door. "Hey, if the colonel has been out of contact since last night, how did he give the order to release Missy Malden from house arrest?"

"I . . . didn't even know he had done that. The last time he was here, I overheard a conversation saying that he was going to keep her under house arrest for her own protection. It seems strange that he would change his mind."

Conrad's brain started whirring. "Remind me of the special investigator's name and contact details?"

"Yes, his name is Major Harris Bowman, and I have his number right here. Would you like me to get him on the line?"

Conrad affirmed and they waited for the major to pick up.

"Major Bowman, this is Lieutenant Colonel Conrad— we spoke briefly yesterday about Major Malden. I heard you gave the order for her to be released from house arrest."

"I did. But the order came from Colonel Cameron."

"Well, that's the thing. No one has seen Colonel Cameron since last night. When did you speak to him?" *Please don't let this be anything.*

"I didn't speak to him at all. He sent me an email."

"You never actually spoke to him?"

"No."

"What time did he email you?"

"Let me check." There was a pause. "I opened it first thing in the morning, but he sent it...let me see...at ten after midnight. It says he sent it from his iPhone."

"Okay, thank you for your time." He was about to hang up, when he heard him say something else. He put the phone back to his ear. "Excuse me?"

"Is there anything you're not telling me? Should I be worried about this?" Major Bowman asked.

"I don't know, but no one's seen Colonel Cameron since yesterday evening. He seems to be AWOL today."

Bowman groaned but said nothing.

"Look, I'm slightly concerned that Colonel Cameron wanted to leave Major Malden in custody to protect her and then changed his mind at midnight last night. Take down my number, just in case you need to get hold of me." He recited his cell phone number and then hung up. He raised his eyebrows at Captain Moss. "I don't know what would have made him change his mind at midnight last night. Do you think there's a chance that something's happened to him?"

The assistant shook her head. "Again, you didn't hear this from me, but he had a date last night. I'm not going to go around raising the alarm if he's getting lucky for once."

Conrad tried not to smile. He hoped that was all it was. But he was sure Cameron wasn't the type to just sleep in when the base was going to shit and two pilots had gone missing.

"I don't know," Conrad said. "Has he ever been this far off grid before?"

"I've only been here six months. But in that time, no."

Well, if she knew he had a date, maybe she knew who the date was. He asked.

"Yeah. Again..."

"Yes, yes, I didn't hear this from you," Conrad rattled off, becoming slightly exasperated.

"Okay, she used to be a pilot. She used to fly here at Red Flag. I think that's where they met."

That put Conrad's mind at rest. At least he was out

with someone who was ex-military. He nodded and took his hat out of his pocket. "Okay, thanks for your help, and if you see it in yourself to slide me up a few numbers from twenty-eight, I'd appreciate it."

"You betcha," she said, writing on her notebook.

Conrad turned to leave and paused in the doorway to let somebody else pass down the narrow corridor.

"Oh. I don't know if it makes a difference, but his date? The ex-military one? She now works for TGO. That's why she's here at Nellis."

Conrad blew out a breath of air. He didn't know it made a difference, but his mind wasn't quite as at rest is it had been before. Half of him felt as if he should stay, bring the captain a cup of coffee, and try to find out every single thing she knew. But the other half of him wanted to find Missy, and that was the half that won.

When he didn't find her at the old barracks pseudo-jail, nor the barracks she'd been staying in previously, his heart rate started getting the better of him. Nothing was normal.

The fact that he was worried about Missy, while on a freaking military base, showed just how far the situation had degraded. He had no idea who the ranking officer was on the whole base, and the flight and maintenance crews who had assembled as teams to participate in Red Flag seemed to be turning on each other in an information vacuum.

And he couldn't find Missy. And he didn't even know

if she'd been legitimately released. And if she hadn't been...who had given the order? And why? God, he hoped it was a friend of Missy's who had persuaded Cameron to send the email. The alternative was that someone else sent the email and either had Cameron's phone or had just made the email appear as if it was him. Either way, those two options suggested that someone wanted Missy out of custody for nefarious reasons.

He started to run through the barracks and dorms, asking passersby if anyone had seen her. No one had. His reflexes were on super-high alert with the crisis at hand. It was as if he were in the cockpit and trying to think two steps ahead of an unseen enemy.

That was why when he eventually saw her, doing laps on the track, he was hyper-alert to the people around her. Everyone on or near the track was in military PT gear, which meant they weren't TGO, which seemed to be the common factor linking all the fucked-up shit that had gone down over the past day. If he never saw a stupid TGO key ring or branded USB drive again it would be too soon.

He slowed down as he reached the track. He was suddenly alarmed at seeing her. What would he say to her? Should he tell her that he wasn't sure that Colonel Cameron had in fact ordered her release? Would it make her paranoid? Was honesty the best policy? Was it safer to tell her? He slowed right down to a crawl. He should have thought this through. He hadn't.

He spun around so she wouldn't see him and walked to

the other side of the road and sat on a small wall where he could still have eyes on her.

He needed to think. Not just about the danger he may or may not have made up in his head, but about them. About their future. Yes, he wanted to fly with her, but he just wanted to be with her too. How could they date if she was on the other side of the country? How would he get past the little he knew about her, and how would she get past his lies? He needed to come up with a plan.

That was it. He would come up with a plan and...no. That was a terrible idea. She had to decide what she wanted to do, and it was up to him to persuade her. But for now, all he had to do was keep her in sight.

CHAPTER SEVENTEEN

For the first time on a military base, Missy felt nervous walking in the dark. She couldn't tell if this whole business had made her paranoid, or if she really was being stalked. She quickened her pace, unsure of whether to stay in the shadows, where she was harder to see, or walk deliberately in the dim pools of light from the streetlamps.

She'd run too long, then she'd spent too long at the gym, and then too long in the shower. If she were being truthful, she was avoiding Conrad. She had no idea what to say to him. All she'd come up with in the hours she'd been working out was to try to be casual when she saw him next.

Their best possible outcome was a clean break—just as she'd planned all along. Sure, the sex was amazing, and she almost felt as if she were a little closer to him in the past few days. But Conrad had done what Eleanor or any other good friend would have done for her. Minus the sex, that was.

Missy wondered if the lockdown was over. She wondered how soon she could leave and never look back. She also wanted to confirm with her squadron commander that she was leaving. She just wanted normal back. Normal was good for her. Normal worked. Normal didn't bring those weird feelings back, the ones she hadn't felt for over a decade.

She slowed down as she passed the track again and the little playground in the corner where she and Conrad had...played? She stopped and looked at it, wondering if anyone had seen them there.

A sharp snap pierced the cool air. She jumped and looked frantically around her.

There was no one there. She was sure it had come from the wooded area in front of the playground. Was it an animal? Someone watching her? Her head told her to run, but her body wanted her to find out what—or who—was there.

She looked around for anybody nearby who might go with her. But there was no one. And she was smart enough to know that the kid who investigated the sound was always the first to die in horror movies. She was *not* going to be that too-stupid-to-live heroine. She put her hands on her hips and glared into the trees, squinting to see if she could catch any movement. Nothing.

Shrugging, she turned and took a light jog up the road to the other side of the track, which was the easiest way to get back to her room.

Just as she was passing the upper bend of the track, another, much louder crack echoed around her. It sounded like the small-arms fire they used to take in Afghanistan. Iced adrenaline pumped through her as she powered down the road toward the houses that the Nellis-based officers lived in.

"Get down!" a voice yelled just as she reached the first door.

She spun around as a bullet missed her face by centimeters. She immediately hit the deck.

Conrad slid down alongside her.

"What are you doing here?" she gasped.

"Following you," he replied, trying to turn around to face the road without raising his profile to whoever was shooting at them.

"That's not creepy at all." She slid closer to the door and kicked out, hoping someone would let them in and give them cover.

The door opened, and to Missy's horror a little girl stood there, barely more than seven years old. "Get down! Get down!" Missy yelled.

The girl didn't move. Missy launched herself up and pulled the girl down, landing in the hallway of the house. Thankfully adult footsteps came running.

"What the hell is—" a man said.

"Shooter!" Missy gasped. With relief she felt the little girl being pulled out from under her. "Call the MPs," she said.

But the man was already dialing. He identified himself as a chief when someone picked up.

"Conrad, get in here," she yelled through the still-open door.

He crawled in and kicked the door shut. "Stay away from the windows," he instructed the man. "Is there anyone else in the house?"

Another bullet hit the door.

"Get down!" Conrad yelled.

Everyone hit the deck, and silence reigned. Until the unmistakable sound of approaching footsteps got louder and louder.

Chris Grove had been watching the fucking tragedy of having an amateur try to do a hit. He couldn't wait to report this shit show to Danvers. But now all he could do was get the job done.

He watched as Mr. Amateur Hour threw the rifle down in the wooded area next to the track and ran for it. Man, he would have a lot to answer for in the morning. Unless he caught up with the jackass himself.

With ice-cold blood slowly pumping through his body, he took his sidearm out and chambered a round. His heart rate barely rose at all. In fact, there was nothing that brought more calm to his body and brain than the prospect of killing. And from what he saw, he could get two for the price of one right here. That dumb-ass pilot who kept following Major Malden around would get a taste of what a real killer could do. Not just some jock who pushes a button at twenty thousand feet in the air and goes home to report his "kills." Fuck that pussy-ass shit. Grove was the real deal.

He approached the house they'd disappeared into. The MPs were on the far side of base, unless one just happened to be out patrolling, and with TGO taking over the base, he could allow for an extra few minutes of confusion. He could count on five minutes. If he was lucky, maybe eight.

As he reached the door, the outside light flicked off. They were clearly expecting him. But he knew that firearms were not permitted in base housing, so as long as he was fast, there was no danger for him. He listened but heard nothing.

Then he heard giggling. *What?* His head twitched to the side. Had it come from the side of the house? Did they really not think he was coming?

He put his back to the outside wall of the house and cleared his range of vision. He spun around the corner, his gun up and ready.

There was no one there. But he heard another fucking giggle—this time with an accompanying murmur. This time from the back of the house. Did they not fear him? What the fuck was going on? Anger rose inside him. He was going to kill them all. Then maybe their neighbors, even the fucking dogs if they had them.

He sprang around the back corner of the house, into the backyard. He saw a figure in the shadows. He slid into a brilliant shooter stance, just like he'd had drilled into him by the bastard sergeant at the range, and his trigger finger twitched with anticipation.

"Dude. Are you really that easy to fool?" a female voice came out of the dark. Clear and strong.

It must be Major Malden. He spun around and with his eyes half closed, used his hearing to identify his target.

"Cat got your tongue?" the voice said again.

There, he had her. He squeezed his trigger, but before the shot could be taken, he took a hard blow to the head. He didn't go down, but lights flickered in his eyes. He shook his head to rid himself of the pain and fuzziness.

He turned to fucking annihilate his attacker. But the man was too close to raise his weapon again. It was that fucking pilot. He could take a pilot with one hand tied behind his back.

Missy saw the man turn to Conrad, and she ran out of the trees holding a shovel that she'd found in the yard. She and Conrad had made the decision to take the fight outside, away from the family.

She charged at him, knowing full well that if he saw her, there was no way she'd be able to dodge a bullet. The only thing going in her favor was that at night, people tended to shoot higher than their target. And she was pretty short, all things considered.

The man punched Conrad in the face and he staggered backward from the force. Missy saw the man raise his gun. She raised the shovel above her head and whacked it down on his arm as soon as she was close enough. He howled and dropped the weapon. It disappeared into the dark grass. At least that had evened the odds.

Her heart pounded from fear as the man swung around toward her. It was Grove. The man she'd picked out of the contractor passes. She'd been right. She dodged backward, just out of his swinging range, but although his face said her time was up, as he raised his arm to hit her, his face contorted in agony.

Grove looked at his own arm, hanging at an awkward angle. Jesus.

She'd broken his arm.

Cool.

"Hey, dickhead," Conrad said.

Grove looked around, and Conrad floored him with one punch to the nose. He crumpled and lay still.

Missy made sure that he was actually out cold and not faking, and then stood up, breathing hard from fear and relief.

They stood over his prostrate body and looked at each other. She kicked his leg, but he didn't move.

"I want to kiss you, but we need to get inside," Conrad said, grabbing some garden twine and binding Grove's legs and hands together.

"What do you mean? You got him," Missy said, wanting it all to be over, really, *really* wanting it to be over.

"The guy I saw was taller and had a long gun, like a rifle. Not a sidearm," Conrad said, ushering her to the patio doors. He knocked on the glass, and the chief let them back in.

"Against my better judgment," he said.

"I appreciate the vote of confidence," Missy said.

"Back in the hallway. I don't want anyone near the windows. I think there was a second man," Conrad explained to the chief.

Both Missy and Conrad were sitting on the floor. They heard nothing. "Maybe there wasn't a second guy?" she said, starting to get up, but the man of the house motioned her to sit back down. "I'd like you two to stay there until we figure out what's going on."

It was a reasonable request. "My name is Major Missy Malden. I'm a weapons officer on the F-15s, and this is Lieutenant Colonel Conrad, one of the pilots in my squadron."

"Sorry, ma'am, but my family is in the house. I'd feel more comfortable if you stay put until the MPs arrived."

Missy caught sight of the little girl at the top of the stairs. "No, we completely understand."

Conrad made a face at her as if he did not understand at all. Missy squinted her eyes at him. She still wanted to know why he was following her but suspected it wasn't a conversation to have in front of the family.

"Did you see the other guy?" she asked Conrad.

"I saw someone with a rifle by the track. But it was too dark and he was half camouflaged by the trees. I saw a muzzle flash, though," he said, before swallowing hard.

"Did you think I was going to die?" She lowered her voice to a whisper. "Are you going to cry?" She bit her lower lip, as if trying not to smile.

Joking was the last thing she wanted to do, but it was the only thing that would make her feel better. Their constant banter in the aircraft had taught her that. Well, he had taught her that. Humor kept the shadows at bay. When they'd been under incoming fire, he'd always talk to the bad guys as if they were naughty children. He'd make her laugh to forget that they could die at any moment.

He was cool like that.

A warning siren sounded outside the house, and a tinny, robotic voice came over the base speakers. "Shelter in place. Shelter in place."

"I guess we're on lockdown again." She shook her head. "I can't believe how hard we worked to get selected for Red Flag, and I can't believe what utter shit it's been."

Conrad grinned, his blue eyes crinkling. "Yeah, man. I had to spend so much freaking time with you. What a pain in the—"

"Ahem," the man said, looking meaningfully up at his daughter.

"—neck that was." He pulled an apology face. "Sorry to interrupt your evening with this...mess, err...?"

"Chief. I'm Chief Whitney of the Fifty-Third Test and Eval."

"Sorry, Chief. I should have figured that a kid could

have answered the door. I was just looking for shelter and I guess my brain fritzed," she said apologetically.

The chief relaxed a bit. "This happen to you a lot?"

She pulled a face. "Not until we arrived at Nellis. Everything went to shit after the first mission."

"Well, not everything," Conrad complained.

She couldn't believe his nerve. "Mostly everything."

The chief nodded and sat on the stairs. He sighed. "Not going to lie: I wish we weren't here right now. As far as I can tell, the ranking officer on base is missing, his vice is away at Fort Drum, and no one seems to be in charge since the general left. I hear they're sending us the base commander from Creech, but he'd only just taken over from the previous commander on Tuesday. So..."

There was a knock at the door. "Chief? Is everything okay in there?"

"This is Chief Whitney. Everything is okay. I'm opening the door." He slowly pulled open the door to three MPs with their weapons drawn and aiming into the house.

Missy and Conrad stuck their hands right up. The chief didn't, and obviously the MPs knew him, as they immediately holstered their handguns.

Missy was just happy they weren't the ones who'd taken her and Conrad into custody two days ago.

"We found the guy out back. He's groggy but won't speak to us. Anyone tell us what was going on?" a female MP said.

Missy raised her hand.

"No need to put your hand up, ma'am. Just tell us what you saw."

"I was returning to my barracks, coming from the gym, when I heard a snap in the woods by the track. I assumed it was an animal or something, but somehow I got a little freaked out by it. So I started running down here, toward the houses, when he"—she pointed at Conrad—"shouted at me to get down. I turned around, and a round flew past my face. I got on the ground, Conrad joined me, and then I tried to knock on this front door to find shelter. The guy at the back is called Chris Grove and is a TGO employee. Major Bowman from the OSI has been looking for him, and he tried to shoot us. But Conrad thinks there was a second shooter."

Conrad nodded. "She's right. I saw a man with a rifle in the trees. It was too dark to see a face, but he was about five-ten and average build. That's all I can tell you. I was more concerned that he was going to pop my...weapons officer here." He pointed at Missy.

"Were you running together?"

"No," Missy answered, folding her arms, waiting to hear exactly why he was following her.

"I was looking for her," Conrad said easily, with a shrug.

Missy rolled her eyes, and the MP didn't seem to know what to make of it. "So you're the only one who saw a man in the shadows with a gun?"

"Yeah. But Grove—the guy outside—is only like five-seven. I'm pretty sure he wasn't the one with the rifle."

And that was that. The MPs made a cordon around the chief's front yard, hauled Grove off to the MPs station, and told everyone to go back to their homes and to make themselves available tomorrow for questioning.

They apologized again to the chief and took their leave. They were stopped in three places in the short mile it took them to go back to Conrad's lodging. The MPs had set up blocks on every pathway, road, and alleyway to check IDs and search bags.

She would have felt safer if not for Conrad's conviction that there was a second gunman. She was so ready to leave Nellis for good.

CHAPTER EIGHTEEN

Conrad didn't want to let Missy out of his sight. Not ever. They stopped to pick up her backpack from the barracks, and he carried it for her to his room. He wasn't leaving her in dorm rooms when someone had tried to shoot her.

When they got to his room, he shut the door behind them and engaged the lock. "You nearly died out there today," he said, dumping her backpack on the floor.

She took a breath. "So did you. Let's hope it's over now. The MPs would have found someone else if he was there. It's what they're trained for."

He put his hands on her shoulders. "I know what I saw. It wasn't waving fucking tree branches. It was a man, dressed in black, with combat makeup on, aiming a long weapon at you. And the muzzle flash I saw wasn't fireflies. You trust me to pilot your aircraft—you should trust my eyesight too."

She nodded. "Sure. But what you're saying is someone wants me dead. And that's not comforting at all. I think I'd rather have thought that Grove was the shooter and he's safely in custody. But thank you anyway."

He gave a short laugh. "I'll never lie to you again, even if you act like a crazy person and refuse to believe me. Deal?"

"When you put it like that...," she said, rolling her eyes.

There was a pause, as she noticed that he was standing in front of her. He wanted her so badly. The adrenaline was only just starting to dissipate, and he was under the full realization that he had nearly lost her entirely. In his heart, he hoped that he had saved her from being shot by running down the road. He hoped he had spooked the gunman badly enough to throw off his aim. But it was still a close call.

Too close.

He was about to ask if he could touch her. Make love to her. But before he could, she reached for him. She held her arms out to him, a frown wrinkling her brow. Her chin wobbled, and he grasped her to him, holding her tight against his chest, feeling her choke out a sob.

He sat on the bed and pulled her into his lap. As he cradled her, he realized that he would have given anything to protect her. Even his life. On the battlefield, that was a given. But on home ground, he'd never expected to feel that way.

These last few days had blown his mind. He understood a lot more and a whole lot less since Missy had been in his bed.

He pulled her face from his chest. She fought him, as if

she didn't want him to see her crying. But he made her. "Don't hide from me. Don't hide what you're feeling. It's totally understandable, and if I wasn't such an incredibly manly man, I'd be bawling my eyes out too. It's one thing to be shot at in a plane, and a whole other thing when someone is aiming at you personally. And it *was* personal. Someone tried to hurt you and that makes it personal for me too. So, go ahead. Cry, yell, scream, do whatever you need to do, and I'll be here—okay, maybe taking a video of you for YouTube—but I'll be here."

She choked out a laugh, as he had hoped she would. "You can never focus your phone right. I'm not scared." But nevertheless, she allowed him to see her face, streaked with tears and dirt from the chief's yard.

She was beautiful.

He leaned down and kissed her. At first he was gentle— offering affection and loyalty. But her hand stretched up and wrapped around his neck, pulling herself up so she could kiss him properly. Her tongue touched his and ignited a flame deep inside him. Before he could react, she was pulling at his T-shirt, trying to get it over his head while they were still kissing.

He pulled away from her mouth for a second and yanked his shirt off. As he did, he caught sight of them in the mirror set into the wardrobe doors on the other side of the room. She bent her head to kiss his chest, and for a moment it felt as if he were watching other people. Under normal circumstances, it might have aroused him further, but no. It amplified the barriers that had always been between them. Him never being honest about his feelings, her never talking about her past, and now the sex they had shared seemed to have placed another kind of barrier between them.

It was as if they were people acting in a play. Or maybe it was just a dream. A dream in which he was trying so hard to reach her but couldn't.

He closed his eyes and shook his head. The last few days had fucked him over. His life had been squared away—compartmentalized like a stack of Jenga blocks. When Missy announced she was transferring, it was like she'd pulled out a foundational piece. Then she'd been accused of sabotage and shot at. His whole world felt as if it were teetering on the edge of chaos.

He was falling, and Missy was the only thing that made sense to him.

"What are you thinking?" Missy whispered.

He looked at her to find her staring with a puzzled expression on her face.

"I was thinking about you. I was thinking that my life has changed in every way possible since the day we arrived here. We live our lives knowing that everything can change in a split second, especially doing what we do, but when we're here on the ground, in the U.S., you don't think it will happen. Until it does."

Missy knelt on the bed and ran her fingers slowly through his short hair. "I changed everything, didn't I?

If you'd competed here with Captain Michaels, nothing would have changed for you. Nothing at all."

"I certainly wouldn't have slept with him, that's for sure. But the funny thing is, the thought of going back to the way everything was is not appealing at all."

"It sounds like you need a drink," she said with a pained smile.

"Right now, I just need you."

"I'm here," she whispered again, running her hands slowly across his chest.

He closed his eyes, wanting to remember everything, fearful that this would be the last time he would see her. He put his hands over hers and opened his eyes. They met hers in the mirror, but this time, the desire in her expression told a different story.

He stood and turned to the bed, wrapping one hand around her neck and dragging her toward him. She knelt up as he kissed her, as deep as he could drive into her mouth. He wanted to absorb her or fill her. He dragged off her T-shirt and bra, lowering his lips to her breasts as soon as they were free. She moaned and held his head there. While biting her nipples into hardness, he imagined her watching him in the mirror.

His fingers splayed across her collarbone, reveling in how small she was under his hands. They could span her chest, and her waist, and nearly her hips too. She felt both fragile and strong under his touch.

Heat rose through him, robbing him of rational

thought. His instinct kicked in, and his instinct told him to consume her. He pulled down her shorts and panties in one tug. His fingers ran straight through her wetness, to her clit. No teasing, no waiting, he just wanted to hear the pleasure in her throat. It was like a shot of heroin every time he heard her moan.

He slipped two fingers inside her, closing his eyes as he felt her heat surround him.

"I need you," she said on a shaky breath.

"I'm never going to stop needing you," he replied.

She withdrew from him, far enough that she could stop kneeling and actually pull off her shorts and panties. And then she was naked in front of him. "I want you here," she said. "Like on the picnic table, but this time I want to see you."

He swallowed as she walked over to the mirror and looked back at him. He kicked off his shorts and stood behind her, with his hands on her shoulders. He ran his hands down her arms and then stroked down her back. Her tan skin was soft and smooth beneath his fingertips.

Her face transformed in the mirror as he reached around and stroked her breasts. Her eyes fluttered closed for a second, and when she opened them, they were filled with need.

Her nipples hardened under his touch and a flush appeared on her chest and face, making her eyes seem made of glass.

She arched her back, so her ass pushed back into his

hard-on. He pushed back, holding her hips to his. With her body now against his, he slid his hands down her stomach and straight to her pussy. He put one finger on her clit and stroked, using her own wetness as a slick lubricant. She leaned back on him and gasped.

Watching her body in the mirror as it responded to him, with her gaze on his, did away with the barriers he imagined earlier. When she was looking at him, there was nothing between them, nothing at all.

Slowly she bent from her waist and put her hands on either side of the mirror, offering herself to him. From behind, he could see everything. Her ass, her pussy, and her clit.

He dropped to his knees and licked from her clit to her ass and back again. Missy moaned and bent even farther forward to allow him more access. He licked again, and again, until his tongue just flicked at her clitoris.

"I want you inside me when I come," she whispered.

Her words burned through him, setting his soul on fire. He stood and slid inside her, holding her ass to him and reveling in the tight heat around his dick. He held still and put one hand on her hips, holding her firmly to him, and with the other hand between her legs, stroked her. She took one hand off the wall and started stroking her own nipple.

He fought every cell in his body that wanted to ram inside her and watched as they both stroked her to orgasm. He felt it first, her muscles spasming around him as she came, squeezing him tight within her.

As her climax abated, he slipped on a condom and moved her closer into the mirror, so she barely had to bend at all. He held her around the waist and held her gaze as he thrust inside her. His torso was against her back, her head just about leaning on his shoulder.

He held her tight with both arms, barely moving away from her with each thrust. Just as he thought he was managing his orgasm, she placed both her hands on her breasts and squeezed her nipples between her fingers. She moaned and pushed harder against him.

At the perfect vision in front of him, he lost any semblance of control. His balls tightened, and he came in three long, hard pulls.

She will always be a part of him now. He couldn't imagine doing anything in his life without her by his side.

They stared at each other in the mirror for what felt like a whole minute. He wanted to tell her that he'd give up everything to be with her, but he knew she wouldn't let him. He wanted to tell her that he'd been in love with her for two years, but even to his ears it felt like he was pressuring her.

He had no words that could make her stay.

CHAPTER NINETEEN

She woke at 4:00 a.m. Although they'd said everything and nothing already, she wasn't going to make the mistake of leaving when no one would see her again.

Missy took her phone from her backpack and remembered that she'd turned the sound off when she was being held at the old barracks.

A base-wide text message popped up saying that the lockdown had ended at zero two hundred that morning.

She took a breath and opened her Expedia app. Within six minutes she had a flight booked for Florida. She'd already decided to go there directly. She was sure that if she returned home with Conrad, he would persuade her to stay with him. Either for the sex or her weapons skills. And she didn't want to stay for either of those reasons. But the sex, she was afraid, would persuade her every time.

She would ask one of her girlfriends to supervise the military removal people who would descend soon enough to pack up her belongings.

A clean break was the best option. She got up and went to the bathroom to shower and by the time she came out,

Conrad was already awake, understanding in his eyes.

"You're leaving. You got a text while you were in the shower reminding you to check in for your flight." He briefly held up her phone that she'd left on the bed.

"Yep. I'm heading directly to MacDill." She wasn't going to apologize for her decision, nor explain it. He would move on, as he always did.

"At least we can share a cab to the airport."

"You're leaving too?" she asked.

"There's nothing keeping me here. The exercise has all but been abandoned, and I just want to go home. Back to some kind of normality." He laughed. "They always say exercises can be more dangerous than the reality of war. I'm beginning to think they're right."

Missy laughed. They had been through some interesting times. Good war stories that would keep people amused, and shocked, at dinners for the rest of their lives. It felt strange to be saying goodbye to all of that, and even stranger to be saying goodbye to Conrad.

She'd loved him for so long. She could actually put that into words now. Because leaving him was horrible, but staying and being replaced by another woman would be worse. And whatever you could say about Missy's life, she was great at self-preservation.

And that made her ask, "Do you think that guy last night was really after me?"

Conrad sat up. "I don't know. I think this year's Red Flag was so fucked up, it's impossible to say."

"Eleanor texted me yesterday. I sent some stuff to the hospital for her." She smiled. As she was about to tell him what she said, her phone beeped with an email. She grabbed it and read it, scrolling down at the information. "It's from Bowman. They've made an arrest."

"What do you mean?"

"The guy I identified as being the person in the hangar was arrested, with the approval and help of TGO. The CEO—Danvers—said he was unhinged. That he tried to kill Eleanor and the British pilot. The CEO apparently thought he was doing a favor to a troubled ex-military guy by hiring him, but that he had been in the process of firing him for a series of bad judgment calls. He confessed to trying to get rid of Eleanor and the Brit, because they had fought with him in a casino a few nights previously. He said he'd been drunk and they'd attacked him. So, he dicked with their aircraft." She looked over at him. "Obviously I'm paraphrasing there. Wow. That's a whole other level of unhinged. Talk about bad judgment calls."

A load lifted from her shoulders. A weight of tension she hadn't really realized she'd been carrying. She giggled. "I was nearly put away for espionage."

"What do you mean *nearly*? You were. I had to break you out. I will always be the one who broke you out of jail."

He was already thinking in terms of memories. She had made the right decision. She smiled, trying not to let a hint of sadness through. "Yes. You will always be that guy."

*   *   *

Conrad watched as she put her stuff together. It felt as if she were packing pieces of his heart in various zip pouches and pockets to her backpack. All this time he thought he'd locked away his emotions. He was the nerves-of-steel pilot. But maybe she'd had his heart all along anyway. He was kind of okay with that.

He couldn't ask her to stay and put her career on hold for him, and he knew that offering to move, or even quit the air force, would put way too much pressure on her.

If only they'd started this months ago. If only they'd gotten together gradually, so they would have been able to figure everything out as they went along. But instead they had come together like a lightning strike, wrecking everything it its path.

They caught a cab to the airport, and an alien feeling of loss came over him. Her decision to go to MacDill was her rejection of him and their life together—such as it was. He wasn't going to badger her into making a different decision. He wasn't going to beg or tell her how he felt about her, because clearly, despite all they'd gone through, this was something she had to do for her own career. He had to respect that.

Neither of them checked in bags for their respective flights, so they went through security together and sat at her gate since her flight would be the first to depart.

They waited in silence, until the last people had boarded her flight. He stood up and held his hand out to her. She took it and stood next to him toe to toe. "I guess this is it, then," he said, wanting to lengthen the seconds out by days.

"I'm going to miss you," she said. Then she raised her eyes to the ceiling and continued. "I'll miss some things, at least."

He put a hand over his heart. "Only some things?"

"Well, I won't miss the morning-after stories of all your conquests, all the fajitas you've eaten, and their rating out of ten, nor will I miss you bailing on every social occasion. But I will admit that there are some things I will miss now that I didn't even know about before." She bit her lip and gazed at him, her eyelashes fluttering.

His heart sank. She really had believed him every time he talked about the imaginary women he'd been with. But he couldn't blame her because that's what he had intended. That was his excuse for not hanging out with her, his way of ensuring that she never looked at him the way she had the past three days. Because he would not have been able to resist her. And would never have been able to walk away. He still wasn't, which was why it was best that she was doing the walking.

"I'll text you my new details when I get there," she said. "Maybe you can come for a visit sometime?"

That was a bad idea. A bad, bad idea. "I'd like that." Yeah, this was never getting any easier. He took her other hand and kissed her gently on her lips. Their last kiss. "Don't forget me now."

She frowned. "I'm sorry. What did you say your name was again?" She winked at him.

He shook his head. "So hurtful. So, so hurtful."

She picked up her backpack, took a boarding card from her pocket, raised her eyebrows. "See ya."

He nodded once in reply and watched her go. She disappeared onto the walkway and out of his life. He sat down again, watching the workers outside move around the plane. He wanted to sing some power rock ballad about a broken heart. He was in his world, and all the workers were in theirs. He wanted to rip that plane to shreds like he was the Hulk.

But he knew he had to get his shit together and move on. He stood, grabbed his bag, and rolled his neck around on his shoulders, trying to ease some of the tension.

Just as he was turning to leave, unable to actually watch the aircraft push back, a man in green shorts and a white button-down ran up to the gate. "Am I too late?" he asked, thrusting his boarding card at the airline employees.

"No, Mr. Janke. You just made it."

Conrad looked at him. Wasn't that the name of the guy who had tried to get Missy to confess?

"It's Colonel Janke," the man complained.

Yes, it was definitely him.

"I'm sorry, Colonel Janke," the employee said, swiping his boarding card. She gave it back to him and he ran down the Jetway. As soon as he was out of sight, the employee rolled her eyes.

I'm with you, sister. Conrad took a beat. That couldn't be a coincidence. Why would a JAG be flying to MacDill? Why would a base JAG be going anywhere?

He tried to walk casually up to the desk. He grinned at the employee. "Hi. I'm Colonel Conrad, but you can call me Mr. Conrad. In fact, you can call me whatever you want to call me."

She smiled slowly and leaned forward on the counter. "Can I call you anytime?" Humor lit her eyes.

He laughed. "Anything, anytime. I just wanted to tell you that we're not all like him. And, man, he was lucky you let him on the flight, right? I mean, it's not your fault he was running late."

"He only decided an hour ago where he wanted to go. Like, his ticket was only purchased at eight this morning."

Eight a.m. was about the time Missy and he had gone through security. It would have only taken him a call to the base travel office to see where she was headed. Cold trickled down his spine. Janke was following her. There was no other explanation.

He grabbed his phone and dialed his number-one speed dial.

"Hi, this is Major Malden. I'm sorry I can't get to the phone right now but if you leave me a message, I'll call you as soon as I can. Thank you."

He looked out the window and saw the plane pushing back. Tension seeped through his body again. He couldn't even fucking remember the last time he was relaxed.

"When's the next flight to Tampa?" he asked his new friend.

Her fingers flew over the keyboard. "The next one leaves in three hours. Are you going to go and have a word with *Mr.* Janke for me?"

"You better believe I'll be having a word with him. Can you get me on that flight?"

Her eyes flirted with him. "I can get you wherever you want to go."

He smiled back her. "I just bet you can."

He handed her his credit card, and she handed him a new ticket. He looked at her name tag. "Thank you, Nancy. It was an absolute pleasure doing business with you."

"Likewise, I'm sure." She went back to her colleague on the other side of the desk.

He watched the plane depart, while committing half of his attention to figuring out how long Missy's flight would take and how soon he would see her again. To be safe, he left a voice mail. Hopefully she would turn on her phone as the plane was still taxiing to the gate when they landed. It would give her time to figure out the safest place to go.

His fists clenched. She had to stop fucking leaving him. Every time she slipped out, left, or sneaked off, something bad happened.

And he couldn't help but notice that Janke was about five foot ten.

CHAPTER TWENTY

Missy landed at Tampa Airport five hours after she had left Conrad. She had spent the flight trying to read, trying to sleep, and trying to muster up an appetite for a soggy meat sandwich and pretzels. She should have known better. No airman worth their salt traveled anywhere without jerky and protein bars. She had neither.

She was trying hard to feel as if this was a new beginning. She knew this new position was the right thing to do. Without Conrad in the pilot seat, she wouldn't miss being in the air. It never felt quite right, though, any time she was at 30,000 feet and Conrad wasn't flying the plane.

As soon as the plane doors opened and she felt the warm, humid air wash through the cabin, she felt like she was in the right place. It was a new day. A new job. And a new state.

She followed the line of people off the aircraft and into the airport. Only after she got to the bathroom did she remember to turn on her phone. One voice mail.

After washing her hands, she tapped the icon to see

who'd called. Conrad's voice halted her in her tracks. The message was full of bad reception static.

"The last passenger on your flight came late. It's Janke, the JAG you told me about. The airline employee told me he'd only booked his flight an hour before departure. Keep your..." Then there was some static and the message ended.

She paced backward away from the entrance of the bathroom and dialed Conrad back. It went straight to voice mail. Damn! *Okay, so maybe Colonel Janke is a Floridian. Maybe he's coming home after Red Flag.* She squinted at herself in the mirror. No. JAGs were assigned to the base, not the exercise. So he must be based at Nellis.

Conrad obviously thought there was something sinister going on. And it wasn't as if she could dismiss it out of hand, given what they've both been through.

She took a heavy breath; she couldn't stay in the bathroom all day. Hopefully Janke was already on his way, but at least she could keep her eye open for him now.

She emerged from the bathroom, trying not to look around her, trying not to catch his eye, if he was there. She walked down the concourse toward baggage claim and ground transportation, first walking slowly and then speeding up before slowing down again and looking in the store windows. It wasn't until she was looking in the window of the National Geographic store that she saw his reflection in the glass.

He was standing on the other side of the concourse with Ray-Bans on, looking at her, thinking that she probably wouldn't recognize him without his uniform. But she never forgot a man who tried to intimidate her.

Fight or flight? Fight or flight?

She turned and walked right across the concourse toward him, not looking at him until she was just a few feet away.

"What a coinkydink! What are you doing in Tampa, *Colonel*?"

His mouth fell open and he fumbled as he took off his sunglasses.

She remained silent, waiting for him to fill in the dead air.

"I...I'm here...I—"

"You're not a very convincing spy, sir. Who sent you?" *Please let it be someone in charge. Someone who sent him to keep me safe for some reason.* It was a wild and ridiculous guess.

"I'm here on vacation," he said, finally finding his authoritative voice.

"Cool. Where are you staying?" she asked.

He just shook his head.

"Wherever you're vacationing, stay away from me or I will call the police." She spun away and walked fast to the ground transportation area. She looked back and found him standing in place, his cell phone pressed against his ear.

She sat in the back of a cab and asked the driver to take her downtown. The car was cool, so she slipped on her hoodie and tried Conrad's phone again. Voice mail. Again.

But then she guessed he was on a flight to Virginia, back to Langley Air Force Base. He'd probably land soon.

What she wouldn't give to have him here with her. Just to be with him.

But no, she had to shake it off and get on with her life without him. Without him. Alone. The thought sent dread through her. Okay, so instead of searching for excitement or positive vibes, maybe she had to go through her own grieving process? She stuck her tongue out in disgust.

"Can you take me to the nicest hotel in Tampa?" she asked the driver.

"Sure. That would be the Kings Castle. It's expensive," he warned.

"Good." That would mean no freaking colonel on a military per diem would stay there. And she didn't care. She had a load of savings that came of being a single officer, with no dependents and no social life to talk of. She even shared ownership of her horses. So, she'd saved a lot.

She checked into the hotel and tried not to wince at the price. Eh, she deserved it. She booked room service with the receptionist and a massage for later. She was looking forward to an early night, with no worries except reporting to base on Monday. She was having a well-deserved vacation full of room service and swimming in the rooftop pool.

Except as good as all that sounded, what was it without Conrad to talk to? To share the experience? To punch his shoulder when he snarked on something. As frustrating as her life had been with him in it, it seemed disproportionately empty now he had gone. Well truthfully, she had gone. She'd gone to reclaim her life, but it felt now as if she had left her life behind.

Everything was so confusing. She had left her job to gain clarity, but it seemed running away brought the same feelings with just a different surrounding.

She took a breath. It had been only a few hours. It might be months before she could claim this new base, and job, as her own. She had to be patient. Live a little.

A few hours later, she stretched out on the bed, wearing the fluffy dressing gown the spa downstairs had given her. She reckoned she had half an hour before her steak and key lime pie arrived. If she was being honest, she could have done with just the key lime pie, but ordering a proper meal made her at least feel as if she had her shit together.

There was a knock at the door. Even better. The earlier her meal arrived, the earlier she could take to her big, white, puffy bed. She raced to the door and peeked through the keyhole. All she could see was a tray with a silver dome on it moving as if it were being held up high by the waiter.

She yanked open the door, her hand already on the folded up $5 bill she had ready in her pocket and a looking-forward-to-pie smile on her face.

What confronted her was not pie, but a black 9 mm pointing at her face.

Shock paralyzed her for a second, and then she tried to slam the door on him. It hit his arm, and he dropped the tray he'd been carrying. She leaned against the door, squashing his arm. "Help! Help!" she yelled, but the sound was muffled by the expensive carpets and thick walls.

Her back pressed against the door, trying to keep him from coming in, his arm bent around the door toward her. Her heart pounded, looking around for anything to use as a weapon.

There was nothing—the room was too big to reach anything. Fear loosened everything in her body, her hands became cold, and her bare feet started to slip on the carpet. Terror zipped through her. If that muzzle managed to point her way, if that man made it into the room, it was basically game over.

She reached for his gun, pushing his arm away from her, but as his arm straightened, her purchase against the door weakened.

An unknown man was trying to kill her? There was no way she was putting up with this crap.

She slid one of her hands down from the gun and used her short nails to rip through his skin. No hesitation. She drew blood the first time.

The man grunted on the other side of the door, but as she'd had to loosen her grip on the gun to scratch him, he used the brief weakness to his advantage and barged the door.

Missy did the best she could. She counted to three and let go of his hand and jumped away from the door. It banged open, and the man staggered into the room, caught off guard. She caught a glimpse of his face. Janke.

She was more than furious and then more than scared. Storming her hotel room with a gun was career ending for him, so she probably wasn't going to be able to talk him out of killing her.

Fight or flight. Fight or flight.

For the first time in her life, there was no upside to fighting. None that her frazzled brain could parse. She dashed for the door that was closing very slowly the way they do in expensive hotels. She managed to get through it, into the corridor, but he was on her immediately, using his height and strength to lift her right off the ground with arms around her waist.

"Help! Fire!" she shrieked as loud as she could. A door banged at the end of the corridor, but no one came to help. He carried her back into the room. She kicked and punched behind her to try to make contact with him, and he threw her on the bed.

He aimed his weapon on her again. "Stay."

She bit her lip to prevent it from trembling. She shook her head. "Why are you doing this?" she asked, horrified at the lack of control she had over her jagged voice.

"I'm being a patriot. Sometimes you have to sacrifice one life to save thousands." He said the words as if he were repeating something he'd heard.

Either way, it didn't sound good. "So, you're going to kill me? What about all the people I've told? Will you kill them to stop them talking too?" Now she was swimming in unchartered waters. She didn't know exactly what had brought him to her, but she was hedging her bets that TGO had something to do with it.

His jaw clenched. "Who have you told? What did you tell them?" He raised his gun again.

"I'm not going to tell you anything!"

Missy took a deep breath and looked for something to use as a weapon. Maybe the phone. Maybe the lamp.

He gritted his teeth. "I'm not playing games here. Tell me who else knows." He pulled the gun back up and aimed it, double-handed—the way they'd both been taught—at her head.

Instinctively she dipped her head down, cowering from the inevitable shot, waiting for the sound of the death shot. Her death. Her life didn't flash before her eyes, only Conrad did. His easy smile, flying with him... The hands clasped in her lap became wet, and she realized she was crying big, hot tears.

She wasn't getting out of this alive. She understood that now. And she wasn't putting the MPs, Bowman, or Conrad in the crosshairs when she wouldn't be around to protect them. She took a deep breath. "How did you find me?" she asked, stalling for time and wondering if it was even worth it.

"Grove put a tracker on you when he met you before.

You probably didn't see it. It just looks like a tiny sticker," he said.

A shiver pulsed down her back at the thought of Grove knowing where she was at all times. And then she realized. That's why she'd been released. They couldn't get to her while she was in custody. They'd only be able to get to her when she was out.

Her head came up, and her back straightened. "Did you try to shoot me last night?"

Janke's mouth twisted. He didn't answer.

Couldn't take failure, huh? "You missed by a mile, man. I hope you never tried out to be a sniper... What an embarrassment that would have been." She shook her head at him, trying to look normal. Trying not to show the terror that was almost controlling her whole body.

He approached her, and she fought the urge to scramble away from him across the bed. Instead of shooting her, or hitting her, he picked up the pad and pen that was by the bed and threw them at her. "Write down the names of everyone you told."

That made her laugh. "Riiiight. And what's the upside of doing that for me?"

"I won't kill you," he said.

No one believed that. She didn't believe it. She just rolled her eyes at him.

"Why are you here?" she asked.

"Major Daniels—Eleanor—told you about the conversation she overheard between her father—the general—

and Mr. Danvers," he said, switching gun hands so he could pull off the messenger bag he was wearing across his chest.

What? "No, she didn't. What conversation?"

Janke hesitated for a moment, tipping his head to one side. "You told the general and Mr. Danvers that you'd seen Grove leaving your hangar and that you knew Eleanor had told him about it, because she told you about their conversation."

He brain clicked one time, and everything fell into place. "Wait. All of this is because I told the general that Eleanor had told me about their conversation? No. She told me she was *going* to have a conversation with him. I barely saw her after that." Only that one time after Missy had been with Conrad. God, she hoped Eleanor was alive.

He paused, then shrugged. "Under normal circumstances, I'd tell you that you need to work on your communication skills, but you probably don't have time now." He pulled out a length of paracord from his bag.

Was he going to tie her up? She tried to play for time...Maybe the real room service would come. "So why would killing me save thousands of people?"

"I take orders. I don't need to see the fine print." He beckoned her with the gun.

She got up slowly, her thoughts now only on Conrad. She should have stayed with him at Red Flag, but she was so eager to flee before she confessed her feelings to him.

Her thoughts flittered away to a life a MacDill that she wouldn't get to enjoy now.

Heat pooled in her gut as he poked her with the muzzle of his gun. "Stop doing that. Just tell me where you want me to go," she snapped.

He backed away from her and opened the bathroom door, taking the fastest look over his shoulder to see what was in there. "This will do fine." He beckoned her again, and when she reached the bathroom door, he handed her the rope. "Do you know how to make a noose?"

"I think she may have just forgotten that I was coming." He rolled his eyes and shook his head, trying to flirt with the receptionist here, as he'd done at the airport. "She probably just checked in, booked a massage, and forgot all about me."

It had taken Conrad an hour and a half to find the hotel she was checked into. She wasn't in base lodging, so he had called every hotel, asking to be put through to her room. He knew she would be looking for a big hotel in the city, so he started with the top ten on a travel website. It had only taken him this long because the fancy-ass hotel she had picked was so expensive, it wasn't even in the top twenty of the most popular hotels. Damn her for switching off her cell phone.

And now he was trying to chat up the receptionist to find out where she was. He'd started off by claiming that he was due to meet her in the lobby, and he had asked the receptionist to call her. But it turned out she had left a do not disturb notice on her phone line and her door. He tried her cell again. It went straight to voice mail.

So it was left to him now to persuade the receptionist to call her room anyway. "I absolutely swear she will not mind if you call through to her room." He slid a folded $20 bill over the reception desk and immediately regretted it when he saw her expression. Yeah, even the most basic rooms here ran around $500, so $20 was probably the equivalent of slipping a maître d' at a fancy restaurant a dollar.

"I'm so sorry. It's all I have. I've just flown in from a war zone, and I spent all my cash on a taxi." He wasn't strictly lying; Red Flag had seemed like a legitimate war zone this year.

Her eyes gave off a suddenly interested air. "Are you in the military?" she asked.

He smiled. "Yes, ma'am, I am. I'm a pilot. I fly fighter jets, and so does my colleague, Missy Malden." He nodded his head back to her computer screen. "I'm just a little earlier than she expected. I'm sure she won't mind you calling."

The receptionist blinked slowly, pushed the $20 back toward Conrad, and picked up her phone. He smiled, but his eyes were on the button she pressed—1856.

The receptionist frowned. "I think she picked up, but all I can hear are sounds." She handed the receiver to Conrad and he listened. It sounded like a struggle. Jesus.

He sprang into action. He dumped his backpack in

front of the reception desk. "Call security to her room. Call the police!" He sprinted to the bank of elevators at the center of the hotel. His eyes widened as the elevators stood resolutely shut.

He couldn't just stand there while she was in danger. He looked for the stairwell, but as his gaze rested on the sign, the elevator pinged open. Two old people stepped out slowly, and Conrad got in. A couple with children tried to get in but he held his hand out to stop them. "No, sorry, emergency."

They looked angry, but they didn't try to force themselves on the elevator with him. His worst nightmare would have been sharing the elevator with a kid who'd think it was funny to hit all the buttons.

It felt like it took five minutes to get to the eighteenth floor, but it was probably only seconds. Long enough, though, for him to think about someone hurting Missy. Or worse, his life without her.

The elevator pinged, and he was out in the corridor before they fully opened. He stopped only to check the location of her room. None of the doors were open, which meant he wouldn't be able to get in. He ran in the opposite direction, looking for a maid. He found one, and with the very force of his expression probably, made her run with him to Missy's door.

He put his finger to his lips. "Shh." He took the card from her and quietly slid it into the lock. He made a sign of a telephone. "Call the police."

She paled and nodded, backing down the hallway and taking out a walkie-talkie from her uniform pocket.

Conrad took a breath and crouched on the floor. With one hand he steadied himself on the doorjamb; with the other, he slowly pushed open the door.

The main room was empty, but all the noise was coming from the bathroom. The door was open and the light was on, and he could see shadows moving and loud bangs. He had planned on closing the door quietly so he could take whoever it was—Janke, he supposed—by surprise. But when he heard the groans and thumps, well. Fuck that.

The door slammed behind him just as he appeared in the doorway of the bathroom. His eyes boggled at the sight. Missy was hanging from the corner of the built-in shower. Rope was wrapped around her throat. She was struggling, trying to get purchase on the glass with her bare feet. Her face was bright red under the pressure. She croaked when she saw him.

Every molecule in his body demanded he save her, but Janke had a gun trained on him.

Conrad just had to get him to lower his guard for a second. Then he realized that his hand was on a towel that was hanging on a hook on the wall. He took it without looking and threw it over Janke's head. In his surprise, he slipped back against the towel heater and slid to the floor, his gun clacking against the tile floor as he braced himself. In the moments it took him to scrabble free from under the fluffy towel, Conrad lifted Missy free and dropped her on the floor of the bathroom.

Janke leveled his 9 mm at him again. Fuck no. He wasn't going to let him get away with that shit. He jumped on him, and the gun, and using the full weight of his body, pinned him to the floor. He could feel Janke trying to wrestle the gun out from under him.

He held him as long as he could, trying to look over to see what state Missy was in. It killed him that he couldn't go over to her. Janke was wrestling so hard that he couldn't even see if she was breathing. Red infused his brain and vision. He punched Janke in the head with one hand while holding his gun hand out of the way with the other.

He rammed his fist down on Janke's wrist and the gun clattered away. Missy moaned, and Conrad spun his head to see her. She was alive.

He felt the rush of wind before he felt the blow to his chin. Conrad fell sideways, fighting the blackness that speckled the edge of his vision. No. He would not pass out. He refused to leave her.

The bathroom was too damn big, with too many sharp corners. He dragged himself up using the door frame, and Janke did the same using the basin. Except his foot slipped in a patch of water.

As soon as Janke went down, Conrad caught hold of his pant leg and dragged him out of the bathroom, wanting to get as much space between him and Missy as possible.

Janke leapt up as soon as he was on the carpet. Conrad deflected two blows to his head, worried that if he took one more, it would be game over for Missy. Where the hell was security?

He stepped back from Janke and kicked him dead in the chest. Air rattled out of the man as he fell backward ... onto Missy, who had just pulled herself up in the doorway.

She crumpled beneath him. Jesus.

With one hand, Conrad gripped Janke's shirt and threw him off her. The colonel scrambled to stay on his feet, and like freaking Jason Bourne, he ran at Conrad, low and hard.

Son of a— Conrad shifted in place, and then side-stepped and threw a punch. Janke's momentum brought his face in contact with Conrad's fist at maximum velocity.

He went down, out cold.

Relief washed over Conrad as his body started to complain at the abuse it had taken. He shook the hand that had taken Janke down and dived for Missy. He took off what was remaining of the cord around her neck and hands and lay her on the bed as gently as he could.

She opened her mouth to speak, but no sound came out. "Don't say anything. Your neck ... " He took a second to get his emotions under control. "It's damaged, probably badly. Just ... don't talk."

Her neck was red and black and was bleeding from

what looked like scratches. She'd probably been trying to loosen the coil to give her some breathing room.

His heart clenched at the sight, knowing he had so nearly lost her. She'd been seconds away. It was only the adrenaline forcing itself around his body that prevented him from bawling his eyes out.

He got a wet towel from the bathroom and put it over her neck, hoping the cold water would help with the inflammation.

There was a noise at the door, and four men dressed in black burst into the room. "Stand back from the bed, sir," the first man said. Conrad was going to resist, but the sight of a Taser on the man's hip persuaded him otherwise. "Please call an ambulance for my friend and the police for this guy, who tried to kill her." He nodded to the still-unconscious Janke. Security put a plastic tie around his wrists.

Missy's eyes were wide and bloodshot, her expression fixed. "Missy. Can you see me?" he asked gently.

She moved her head just a tiny bit up and down. "Okay, it's all over. Janke's in cuffs, hotel security is here, and the police and ambulance are on their way. Okay? It's all over."

A tear leaked out of her eye, and he squeezed the top of her arm gently, not knowing where else she had been hurt. He looked for her wallet and ID and tucked them into his pocket. "I'm going to come with you to the hospital. I'm not going to let you out of my sight, okay?"

She nodded again and closed her eyes.

CHAPTER TWENTY-ONE

When Missy woke up in hospital, she had an irresistible urge to run. But she was in so much pain, she couldn't. It took a while for her eyes to focus in the bright light of the room.

Conrad was sitting next to her, reading a magazine. Her heart calmed immediately. She closed her eyes again in relief. He was here. She loved him.

She opened her mouth to speak but was unable make a sound. Her eyes watered at the pain.

Conrad dropped his magazine at her attempt at speaking. "Don't do that. Your larynx and trachea are really badly bruised. It could take weeks before you're able to speak properly. But I got you this from the shop downstairs." He showed her a My Little Pony notebook and pencil. "It was all they had. But I'm reliably informed that the pencil will write in the colors of the ponies." He shrugged. "I don't know what that means."

Her heart swelled at the thought of him taking advice from a store assistant. Missy was sure that the woman would have suspected that he was buying it for a daughter.

She closed her eyes and dreamed for a second about what it would be like to have a daughter with Conrad. Exasperating, amazing. She managed to stop a tear that threatened to escape her eye.

"Anyway. This is what's happened since you lost consciousness. We have a new commander in chief. Man, you've slept through two whole presidents! Also the Dolphins won the Super Bowl and we're in the middle of a war with France. I've been deployed twice! The wine and cheese made me consider defecting."

Her eyes widened in shock. How the hell long...? And then she saw the twinkle in his eye.

She scowled at him and then opened her hand in a question.

"Only a day. You woke up last night, but they sedated you so they could look down your throat. You can go home today. You just have to do some follow-ups—but I'm sure you can sort that out on base." He'd read her mind. He did exactly what she had been doing to him all these years.

She reached for the paper and pencil.

JANKE?? she wrote, nodding approvingly at the pink and purple letters.

Conrad hesitated. "Swore he was a lone wolf, like Grove. They questioned him and put him back in his cell. And by morning he had hanged himself."

Her mouth dropped open. She didn't know what to say, or write. She wasn't sorry for him at all, and she supposed she should feel bad, but he had tried to hang her, so...

"I know it's a bit weird, but I suggest you don't feel bad. I suggest you don't feel anything. After all, if I hadn't followed you on a long flight, then saved your life like a goddamned hero, he would have hanged you too," he said.

She wanted to laugh at him, but she couldn't.

She breathed out of her nose, as her throat was so sore.

"Open wide, I've got something for that."

She goggle-eyed him.

"No, not that. Jeez. Get your mind out of the gutter. What kind of man do you think I am? It's okay; you don't have to answer that. Oh, I forgot, you can't." He held up a bottle of green fluid. "It's a spray for numbing your pain."

She motioned him to put it all over her.

"It's for your throat. Open." He sprayed the liquid down her throat, and most of the pain disappeared instantly. She could swallow without pain. It was a miracle.

Conrad sat on the side of her bed and held her hand. "It's been a rough few days, but you'll get through it okay. Where do you want to go from here? Back to the hotel?"

She thought about it. The hotel was lovely, although she wondered if she'd ever be able to take a shower there again. She shook her head.

"Base lodging? I made a reservation in case you wanted to go there instead."

She nodded.

"Okay, leave everything with me. I'm going to go get your bags, and mine, come to that, and I'll meet you back here to go to MacDill."

She closed her eyes and nodded. He got up to go, but she grabbed his hand. "Thank you," she mouthed.

"You're my wingman. I'm not going to leave you hanging. Oh, sorry, bad turn of phrase." He winked at her, and she tugged his hand across her so that he bent over her. She kissed him on the lips and let him go.

Conrad went back to the swanky hotel and picked up all their things—the backpack he'd abandoned at the reception desk and Missy's things from her room that a concierge had packed. They also comped her the room, which thinking about it was the least they could do after somehow allowing Janke access to her room. They still hadn't figured out how he'd found her room, or known that she'd ordered room service. Best guess was that he had overheard her ordering when she'd checked in.

He was going to urge them to tell the police when they figured it out, but with Janke dead, he wasn't sure anyone would be investigating too hard. But he did need to call Colonel Cameron and tell him that TGO just tried to kill another airman. He sighed. Not that being suspicious of military contractors was unusual. It just seemed that this company in particular had the wool pulled firmly over everyone's eyes.

On his way back to the hospital, he called Cameron's office and no one picked up, so he tried the guy from Special Investigations. He picked up on the first ring.

"Major Bowman. Have you heard about Colonel Janke?"

Bowman sighed. "No. What's he got his shorts in a wad about now?"

In any other circumstances, Conrad would have ripped the major a new one for disrespecting a ranking officer, but since it was Janke, he let it ride. "He tried to kill Major Malden in Florida."

"What the . . . ?" Conrad could hear him scrambling for something to write on.

"He's dead. The local Tampa police arrested him, and he killed himself in his cell."

"Sweet Jesus. Is the major all right?"

"He tried to hang her, so she's not doing much talking right now; in fact, I'm about to spring her from the hospital and take her on base at MacDill. But in case it helps your investigation at Nellis, Janke told her that he was working for TGO. He didn't explicitly say he was under orders from them, but she strongly got the impression that he was charged with tying up loose ends," Conrad said wearily, more than ready to leave all this behind.

There was silence on Bowman's end.

"Did you get that?" Conrad said

"Yeah, I did. Thanks." Bowman sounded defeated.

"What's wrong?" Conrad frowned. He'd thought that Bowman would be ecstatic to get a bead on TGO.

"It's all hearsay. All we have is someone who says a dead guy told her something. I can't so much as get a search warrant with that." He seemed to shake it off. "It doesn't matter. At least I know what I'm looking for now and who to be suspicious around. Thanks for the info. If I need anything else, I'll get in touch with your local Office of Special Investigations."

No time soon, he hoped as he ended the call.

While Missy had been sleeping off the anesthetic, Conrad had Googled TGO and looked at its board of directors and the think tank that it operated in DC. There were a lot of people way high up in the government that were entangled with TGO, including senators, congressmen, and people in the White House. He wondered how much money TGO paid for those board positions, because all those people also had full-time jobs. Seems like either they weren't doing their jobs as government servants, or they were taking money for doing nothing—except maybe directing Pentagon funds their way.

It was way above his pay grade. He was happy to leave all that palace intrigue alone.

Not that he was 100 percent sure what his pay grade was anymore. In the time it had taken him to fly to Tampa, fight for the life of the woman he loved, and sit by her bedside while she slept, he had realized that his life would be nothing without her in it. It was nothing to do with their professional life. Of course she made him better, but spending that long working almost exclusively with anyone would.

It was her. It had always been her, and now he had

to make his move and make sure she knew it. What she said—or wrote—would determine his future. Because he sure as shit wasn't going to let her out of his line of sight again, unless she forced him to.

By the time he rented a car, got back to the hospital with all their gear, waited for the doctor to discharge her, and pick up meds from the pharmacy, it was getting late.

She sat next to him in the car, with her head back against the headrest and her green spray in her hand. When they finally drove onto the most beautiful military base he'd ever set eyes on, she heaved a sigh of relief. The lodging overlooked the sea, and frankly, the salty air seemed to act like an antiseptic to everything they'd gone through.

"This is nice. No wonder you wanted to live here. Do you have a house on base?"

She nodded, looking out at the waves crashing on the rocks beneath them. "I think so," she whispered. "All instructors do."

He checked her in and helped her out of the car and up to an open walkway that led to the rooms on the first floor.

The room was considerably less fancy than the one she'd had downtown. "Less fancy is good," she said.

He paused, and she put her bag on the bed and turned around to face him. "I'll go then, and—"

A look of alarm flashed across her face as she grabbed his arm. "No. Stay."

"I can't. I mean, I need to have a conversation with you

about everything, but I can't do that if you can barely talk." He took a step toward the door.

She held up a finger and dug in her bag for the damn My Little Pony pad and pencil.

Talk about stalling the momentum. "Look, we can't have a conversation if only one of us can talk. What if I want to shout at you, and then I have to wait five minutes for you to write a message in all caps so I know you're shouting too?"

She held up her finger again as she scribbled on the paper. After a couple of moments, she lifted the paper so he could see it. Kind of.

He squinted at it and stepped away from it, still squinting. "I think you need to use all caps anyway. I can't... what the hell does that even say? There—does that say puppy?"

She shook her fist at him, which was completely adorable. Then she took back her pad and sat at the desk. She was there for a long time. "You see, this is why having a conversation now is ridiculous. Let's just put a pin in this and revisit it tomorrow," he said.

"I'll stick a pin in you, if you don't shut up," she whispered.

"Not to labor the point, but I saved your life yesterday. Don't you go threatening me." In truth, he wanted to get out of there like there was no tomorrow. He didn't want to spend another night with her without knowing that she would be his forever.

He didn't want her to decide today what his fate would be. He wanted more time to have hope, which was the one thing she'd never given him. She'd never inferred or hinted, or even just looked at him as if she wanted him in her life as anything other than a colleague.

Give him just one more night of hope, please.

He opened the room door, and she kicked the trash can hard enough for him to look around again. She was still holding her finger up for him to wait.

He watched as she made deliberate letters on the pad, using God knows how many pieces of paper.

She cleared her throat, and then teared up in pain. He lunged for the spray and handed it to her. She sprayed and took a breath.

She handed him each page one at a time.

If you love me, stay.

Because I love you, even though you are an ASS at times.

And I think we would be good together.

Maybe.

Unless you don't.

In which case, J/K.

?????

With each page, his heart lurched in his chest until the last few, when he laughed. "Okay. I'll stay. I'll give you a little while to sell me on MacDill, and you, of course. But you need to sell hard."

She threw the multicolored pencil at him. He watched it as it sailed by him about a foot from the target.

"And I won't tell people what a terrible shot you are when you're not in an F-15."

"I love you," she whispered.

"I love you too. I think I always did."

Tears appeared in her eyes, and she allowed them to fall unchecked. She held her hand out to him, tears now falling onto her T-shirt. His heart grew by 200 percent as her eyes told him everything he needed to know.

EPILOGUE

One year later

Is it true that you and Colonel Conrad are the ones that the textbook talks about, ma'am?" The young man found the page in their textbook and pointed at it.

The other students groaned. "What's the matter with you?" he shot back at them. "This is all we talk about when we're at the chow hall. I just thought I'd cut to the chase." He turned his attention back to Missy. "People say it was you. That you were the ones who used a supersonic boom to fool the enemy that you were about to drop more bombs when you'd actually run out of missiles?"

Missy smiled at Conrad, who was at the back of the class, leaning against the wall, waiting for her to finish for the day. "Does the textbook have our names in it?" she asked with a smile.

"No, ma'am."

"Then you should probably assume it's classified, and you shouldn't—"

"It was totally us," Conrad butted in. "And the whole thing was Major Conrad's idea." He pointed at Missy. "We were out of weapons, we were running low on fuel and didn't have much maneuverability, and she figured we had one more attempt at forcing them to retreat so our ground troops could regroup." Missy rolled her eyes as Conrad used his hand as if it were his plane. The students' eyes were fixed on him. "So, we banked around the mountain and tripped it up to Mach II, and dropped a *boom* on them that made them think heaven was dropping in on them. They turned around and ran."

"Awesome," the young airman said, nodding. The other students grinned.

"Now, don't you go telling anyone. That's our secret, right?"

"Yessir!" they chorused. Any time Conrad stopped by on his way to pick up their daughter from the base day care, he always managed to derail her class. "Okay, guys, it's nearly four, and it's Friday, so why don't we pick this up next week?"

The officers looked so damn young to her. "Have a good weekend, and if you're drinking..."

Everyone joined in with the instructions she always gave them: "Have a plan to get home."

She nodded. "I'm not giving up my weekend to visit you in the hospital."

They filed out, leaving her and her husband alone in the classroom.

"It wasn't my idea; it was yours," she said, shaking her head.

"No, it wasn't. It *was* you. I remember being skeptical that it would work."

"You and I have very different memories about a lot of things." She smiled.

"Not everything, though," he replied.

She stepped up to him as close as she could without actually touching him, which would be horribly unprofessional. "No, not everything."

He gazed into her eyes with a warmth and an interest that never failed to weaken her knees. From the moment they'd confessed their feelings to each other, it was as if he'd been given permission to get inside her head. He was always asking her opinion on things and figuring out how she felt. It made her feel loved, more than the words, more than the nights they spent trying not to wake Libby up.

She stretched her arms over her head and sighed. "It's the weekend at last."

"And I get you all to myself. Well, me and Libby get you all to ourselves. Beach? Barbeque? Movie and some making out?" he said, slowly making his way to the front of the classroom.

"All of the above, please," she replied, a pure joy rising in her. If she could shoot rainbows out of the top of her head, she would every day. He had given up flying six months before and become the commandant of the intelligence school at MacDill. They shared a beautiful base house overlooking the bay and had slipped into an easy domestic life filled with laughter and wisecracks. And then their daughter had arrived unplanned and desperately adored.

"Come on. Let's break for the border. Grab Libby and make a run for it," she said, closing her briefcase.

"How I wish you were being serious," he replied. "I'd go on the run with you any day of the week. After we retire."

"It's a date."

He opened the classroom door for her, and they both walked slowly into the late afternoon sunshine, toward the childcare building.

Missy's heart fluttered as it did every day when Conrad picked up her baby. The delight on both their faces made her day complete. Made her life complete.

This was her family. The first she'd ever had. And they were freaking awesome.

As they left the building and headed back to their house, he motioned down to his pocket. "I forgot. I have something for you. Can you...I can't..." He was holding Libby with both hands.

She dug in his pocket and pulled out its sole content. Two AA batteries. "Wha...ohhhh," she said with a giggle. She started speed-walking. She shouted over her shoulder. "Hurry up! Don't make me start without you."

The image of him holding their daughter, with the grin he gave, slayed her.

"Right behind you, sweetheart."

Keep reading for a preview of

FREE FALL

Coming in Spring 2018

CHAPTER 1

Colonel Duke Cameron didn't recognize the man who stared back at him in the mirror. What had happened to him? Clean-shaven, pressed uniform, an uncertain look in his eyes—defeated even. Was this him? Or just some sap who'd had the warrior in him snuffed out through a series of promotions?

With every rank attained, it seemed like another little piece of him had been suppressed until he'd become a completely different officer. But now something inside him was fighting to get out.

He was in his final year of running Red Flag. A hefty retirement check was in his sights, along with a brand-new career. Fishing charters maybe. Or being a golf pro. That's what he told himself anyway, but it was becoming more and more obvious to him that he couldn't go quietly into the night; he was a fighter.

It was supposed to be a smooth transition. But this year's Red Flag had become a total fuck-up. It was eating away at him—the lack of control, the loss of the two pilots in a horrible crash on the second day of the exercise. He could feel it roiling inside. He should be out looking for the missing pilots. He should be doing *something*, goddamn it.

He grimaced in the mirror. The special operator in camo face paint bringing the fight to the enemy, the Osprey pilot who executed the most deadly attacks and fearless rescues had become...this. An insipid commander who played by the rules and respected the line of command. And the latter was sticking in his gut like a five-pound wad of chewing gum.

The three-star general who had shown up from the Pentagon had basically given all operational control of the base, and Red Flag, to a third-party military contractor. And here he was, hunched over a sink in the men's room, not wanting to return to his office lest something else happened that would make him feel even more impotent.

Two planes had crashed the day before, and TGO, the contract company that had paid for Red Flag this year, insisted on being in charge of the search and rescue. The general had agreed, which left Duke sitting with his fucking thumb up his own ass while they dicked around, seemingly unable to find two planes and two pilots on a desert range.

He splashed water on his face slowly, wanting to prolong the moment until he had to go back to his desk and answer every call with a weak "I don't know" response. Because he didn't know a goddamned thing. It was like the whole of Red Flag—Duke's whole reason for being at

Nellis—had been taken away from him. His entire scope of responsibility had been reduced to sitting at his desk, wondering what had happened, and being completely out of the loop.

Someone rushed into the bathroom and ran for one of the stalls. He knew how that felt. But anyway, it was a good enough reason to give the poor guy some privacy. Cameron left, and only realized that he'd slammed the door open with such force that it had bounced against the wall when a couple of officers stopped talking and stared at him. He resisted the urge to apologize.

He was losing control of Red Flag, and himself.

He wasn't the squared-away colonel they saw. He wasn't the obedient by-the-books officer he'd accidentally become. He'd never been that. And it was only now—in the face of losing pilots on his watch—that he was able to really see himself for what he'd become.

The bottom line was that the higher up you rose through the ranks, the more you had to lose. He only had two years to go before his twenty years was up. He just had to keep his head down to get full retirement. At forty-three, he'd be able to get another job, and with his military retirement check, be able to live a quiet, easy life.

Back at his office, Captain Olivia Moss jumped up as he entered.

"Sit down, Captain." He'd been trying to persuade her that she didn't have to stand every time he returned to his office, but she was struggling with the lack of protocol he was apt to enforce in his own domain. Maybe because he was a walking contradiction.

"I just wanted to remind you that it's eighteen hundred hours, and you have a date. I wanted to be sure to give you enough warning so you can go home and take a..." Her voice trailed off as if she'd only just realized how inappropriate it would be to talk to a commander about his showering habits.

Then he focused on what she was reminding him of. A date? "What in the hell are you talking about? What date?"

Her face fell, and her gaze dropped to her planner. "Um. You have a seven o'clock date with a Casey Jacobs?"

He took an uneasy breath. "It's not a date," he bit out. "It's an...appointment." At least, he hoped. Maybe he hoped. *Shit*.

Captain Moss frowned. "Oh God. I'm so sorry."

She looked so stricken that he eased up. "It's not a date. She's a retired major. She used to fly MC-130Js out of Germany. I met her a couple of times when we were deployed. And now she works for TGO. My only goal for the meeting is to try figure out where my pilots are." And what else she knew about TGO.

He visualized how she had looked in his office that afternoon. Beautiful as usual, sharp as usual, but with an imperceptible barrier between them. He was sure she knew something about the crash and why her company was taking forever to find the aircraft and the pilots.

He told himself again that it had nothing to do with

the looks they had exchanged when they'd crossed paths in Afghanistan. Nothing to do with the time they'd taken shelter in the same bunker when their base had been attacked by insurgents. Nothing to do with how she'd been his "what-if" person. Nope. Nada.

Captain Moss had been right, however. He did need to get back and shower before he met her at the officers' club. The base was on lockdown; otherwise he'd have been happy to meet somewhere downtown. There was always something to do in Vegas. But this was probably better. More professional.

"Okay, I'm off," he said, locking his office door. "I'm your first call if you hear anything, okay? Gossip, whispers—anything. Got it?"

She looked affronted. "Of course, Colonel. I have some lures out. As soon as my hook tugs, you'll be the first to know."

He smiled. You could take the woman out of Montana, but... "I'm relying on you to reel in a fifty-pounder."

"You got it, boss," she said as he left.

Casey Jacobs had her phone in her hand and was pacing inside her hotel room. She should switch the phone off, right? But maybe her company would get suspicious if she did. Her nerves were wrangling about her as if her aircraft were taking small-arms fire on descent. Her brain was jumping from thought to thought. She had to calm down.

She took some deep breaths and sat on the bed. Then after a couple of seconds, she put the phone in the drawer of the bedside table. It would be better if it rang and she didn't hear it. Less suspicious maybe.

All she'd done was make an innocent inquiry about the equipment on the planes that had crashed, and her world had collapsed around her. If she kept her mouth shut, everything would be okay. Maybe.

Her friend at TGO headquarters had warned her off. Suggested that TGO tapped its employees' phones. Suggested that they sued whistle-blowers. Suggested that when the whistle-blowers committed suicide, that maybe it wasn't exactly suicide. *What the hell had she gotten into?*

But if they had tapped her phone, they would have already heard her panicked message.

What's going on? We have planes and pilots missing, and their last transmissions suggested the same bugs we experienced in our PreCall software. Aircraft overcorrecting, lack of pilot control, radio static. Did we put PreCall on their aircraft? Did they even know? Is that legal? Call me back! We could have killed these two pilots! Call me back!

Even if she didn't know any specifics, she already had the sense that her new company, and her new boss, Mr. Danvers, were somehow above the law. Their letterhead boasted names from the U.S. Senate and the House of

Representatives. From high up in the Pentagon. From the White House.

She had to try to persuade them that she was on board. But her military training—and her honor and integrity—were battling against her survival instinct. She just plain didn't know what to do.

Her company had sued a former whistle-blower for $50 million and won. The man had been close to destitute as the court only allowed him to keep enough money for rent and little else. No one had raised an eyebrow when he'd killed himself. Except now she'd been given reason to wonder. Malcom, her work buddy at TGO, had suggested to her that TGO had ruined him and then killed him to stop him from talking.

Could that happen to her?

The bedside table vibrated, making her jump. She leaned over and opened the drawer, peering in, not daring to touch the phone in case... well, she didn't really know.

The number was a Nellis one. She frowned and slid her finger across the screen to pick up the call. "Hello?"

"Thank God you're there, baby."

She frowned, not being able to place the voice. "Who is this?"

"Really? We flew together in Afghanistan and you don't even remember me? I saved your life." He sounded hurt.

She grinned. "Animal? Is that you?" Relief threaded through her as she sat back down on the bed. He had saved her life, and the lives of her crew. He'd taken out the nest of a surface-to-air missile that had locked on to her aircraft, and then he'd taken out the missile too. He'd been laughing over the intercom as he had performed a maneuver that had seemed to defy physics as he saved them. An American-educated Korean national, he sometimes sounded more of a Floridian than a native Seoulite.

"You know it. How've you been? I hear you defected to TGO," he said. His tone was casual, but there was something tense lying under it.

He stomach clenched again. She took a breath. "I'd never defect." She left it hanging there.

He paused. "Then I'm calling in my chips."

"Your chips?" As soon as the words were out, she knew what he meant.

"I saved you, so you can help me save someone else. Hopefully," he said after a beat.

"What do you need?" she asked, knowing she was already in the hole. They wanted to go search for the missing pilots.

"I need you to get us off base. I hear TGO—not the air force—has it on lockdown," the Animal said.

"I don't know how . . ." Her mind started whirring, and he fell silent to let her think. "How many of you?"

"Eight, give or take."

"Can you tell me what you're planning?" she asked. And then she remembered about her phone. "Oh, wait. Don't even tell me. There isn't enough booze or women on base to satisfy the Animal?"

"Riiiight?" he said, obviously perplexed.

"Let me call you back." She hung up before he could say anything else, and picked up the phone on her bedside table. She redialed the number he had called from. "It's me."

"Okay. Sure you're not in the CIA instead of TGO?" the Animal said, a touch of humor in his voice.

She wished.

"I'm just being careful. As should you. Can you get a minivan from transport and make out like you're all going to party? I'll make sure I'm at the back gate. What time?"

"As soon as possible. It'll take me about fifteen minutes to get a van. Hold on."

She could hear him talking to someone.

"Yeah. Fifteen minutes. Let's make it twenty. I need to pick up some supplies."

"You're going into the desert, aren't you?" she asked. "You're going to look for the two pilots."

"We're going out looking for our friends." Animal's voice was firm and unbendable. "The way we'd go look for you, if you'd crashed out there."

"I know," Casey said simply. She had no doubt about that. And if she were still in the military, she, too, would have busted out of lockdown to search for missing airmen.

She looked at the clock by the bed. Twenty minutes from now would make it ten after seven. She hoped Cameron would wait for her. "See you there."

Grabbing her bag and car keys, she slipped on her

sneakers. She was already in the dress she'd planned on wearing on her date. No. Not a date. Nevertheless, she picked up the shoes that she might put on, to make it feel more datelike. She didn't know. Would strappy sandals make it seem too datey? Would sneakers make her dress look stupid? Urgh. She'll make up her mind in the car.

She ran down the stairs rather than waiting for the elevator and was in her car within five minutes. She drove past the officers' club on the way to the gate, just to see if Cameron was already there. If he'd been waiting for her outside, she'd have stopped to tell him she had an errand to run first.

She parked her car at the visitor center and walked over to the TGO guys manning the gate. When they saw her coming, they ran to the door of the security hut and held it open for her.

"Good evening, ma'am. What can I help you with?" the younger of the two men said.

"My friends want to go out on the town tonight. I told them they could go." She rolled her eyes as if totally exasperated with them.

"I'm afraid the base is on lockdown," the young guy said.

"It's okay, Scott. This is a senior VP at headquarters. She speaks for Mr. Danvers."

The young man looked confused.

"Mr. Danvers is the CEO of TGO, Scott," the older man said, as if he were talking to a kid. He got off his swivel chair and came from around the high desk, shaking his head. "Can't get the staff these days."

She grinned. "We were all new once," she said.

The older man shook his head as if in dismay. "He's not that new," he said dryly.

She handed her TGO ID to the younger security guard and signed a piece of paper on the clipboard he handed over. As she did so, she realized her mistake. Her name was documented now. Danvers would know she'd let the airmen out. There was no getting away from it. She saw a minibus from the air force recreation facility headed toward the gate. It wasn't hard to figure it was them, as they were the only vehicle exiting the base.

"Here they are," she said, trying to inject a cheeriness into her voice when all she was feeling was doubt, bordering on fear. "If you could let them out, and then I'll be following them in my car." She didn't know why that had slipped out, but as soon as she said it, she knew she'd feel safer off base.

She opened the door and breezed out of the security hut. Her car keys in hand, she dashed to her car and pulled in behind the minibus.

The younger guy opened the electronic security gates. She waved at him to thank him, but he wasn't looking at her; he was looking at the old security guard who seemed to be shouting at him. With a radio to his ear, the older guy slammed his hand down onto the control board, and the gate started to close on her.

Adrenaline shot through her. She wasn't stopping. If he'd called it in, she was in deep trouble. She needed to get out, maybe find a lawyer. Hide. She gunned the car, stomping on the gas.

A motorcyclist in black came up behind her. Nope. No way she was stopping. She took one last look at the security man, who seemed to be punching all the buttons on the gate mechanism in fury.

She accelerated through the gate as it was closing, clipping a side mirror off her car. She was free. She took a deep breath. There was no talking her way out of this one. She was on the run now. She just had to keep one step ahead of TGO.

ABOUT THE AUTHOR

Emmy Curtis is an editor and a romance writer. An ex-pat Brit, she quells her homesickness with Cadbury Flakes and Fray Bentos pies. She's lived in London, Paris, and New York, and has settled, for the time being, in Germany. When not writing, Emmy loves to travel with her military husband and take long walks with their dogs. All things considered, her life is chock-full of hoot, just a little bit of nanny. And if you get that reference...well, she already considers you kin.

Learn more at:
EmmyCurtis.com
Facebook.com/EmmyCurtisAuthor
Twitter @EmmyCurtis19